MURDER,
MYSTERY,
MADNESS,
MAGIC, AND
MAYHEM

MISSOURI
AUTHOR
COLLECTION

*Thirteen Selections from the
First Cave Hollow Press
Anthology Contest*

A Cave Hollow Press Book

Warrensburg, Missouri   2003

Murder, Mystery, Madness, Magic, and Mayhem

Cover art and photography by
Georgia R. Nagel and Rose Marie Kinder

Illustrations by Georgia R. Nagel

CONTENTS

MURDER, MYSTERY, MADNESS, MAGIC, AND MAYHEM

When the visions started, they knew
that something had to be done.

FREEZER
Kevin Prufer

They would never have done it under normal circumstances, but, as things were now, they had no choice but to look down at the man on the carpet and say silently to themselves, this is our doing. We did this, and in a way we're the better for it. They thought this quietly, then, sitting on the love seat by the fire, said it aloud. Of course he deserved it, the woman said, whether she really meant to do it or not, to which the man nodded, held his own hands still in his lap, and told her that if it were to happen again, under calmer circumstances even, he wouldn't have moved an inch to stop her. The guy had been a lousy cook.

The lousiest cook they'd had in thirty years. Nosy, dirty, lecherous. A regular nuisance to the household. He was constantly skulking about, and twice he'd made lascivious remarks about the man's wife. He drank too much and he smelled funny. When they'd come home early to find him lounging before the fire in the man's bathrobe and slippers, drinking his brandy, well, that had been the final straw. The more they talked about it, the more the man realized that had his wife not taken the alabaster Pietà to the cook's head he would have done the same. But with something less fragile, the fire poker maybe. Anyway, she had done the right thing, and that was important. And the Pietà didn't suffer a scratch.

But when everything was said and tucked neatly away for the two of them there was still the third party, the erstwhile servant, legs spread on the carpet behind the couch, robe coming undone at the waist. And soon it would be morning, and this was the city, after all. How did one dispose of this kind of thing? We could roll him up in the loveseat, the woman said, rent a U-Haul, carry him out of town. Maybe leave him on somebody's tree lawn even.

But it was the man's loveseat, pale blue and old. It had belonged to his mother. And the dead cook had to be at least six feet long, anyway. The man suggested, instead, that they cut him into medium-sized chunks with the hacksaw. But neither of them wanted that job, and they certainly couldn't get one of the servants to do it, so any plans for burning him like logs in the fireplace, disposing of him in

3

the dispose-all, feeding him piece by piece to the dog were dashed forever.

They played with many ideas, all of them without success. They could make it look like an accident, roll him out the window. But even if they were to carry him up the stairs without waking the maid, the fall onto their front lawn wasn't likely to imitate the damage to the head. They could leave him on the sidewalk, the woman said, this *was* D.C. after all. Terrible things *did* happen here. But really, not on Foxhall Drive. There would be reports, officers, everything. And they couldn't just leave him on the carpet by the fire. They couldn't do that.

So when the man suggested the freezer in the garage, the woman nodded vigorously. They didn't have anything important in there, anyway, she said. A few Low-Cal Gourmet dinners, microwave lasagna, a couple packages of string beans. Nothing that couldn't be eaten right away or transferred to the kitchen freezer.

It was hard work dragging the old man through the living room, across the kitchen floor, out the back door into the garage. They had to back the Mercedes onto the driveway before emptying the freezer.

And there was more inside than the woman remembered: cartons of ice cream, ice-trays, a forgotten bottle of chilling white wine, waffles, frozen steaks, popsicles, and of course the metal freezer-dividers. When it was finally emptied, they both strained their backs heaving the dead man into the giant white box. When they closed the freezer door, stretched, looked down at the fifty-odd pounds of frozen food around their feet, they felt wonderfully satisfied. Dawn was just breaking through the six square garage windows. Waffles for breakfast, the woman said, and popsicles.

They didn't think about the man in the freezer for weeks. The man had work to do, papers to sign, and of course his wife had countless luncheons to attend. She was busy planning the neighborhood ladies' yearly charity event, and had little time to spare.

None of the servants thought to ask about the whereabouts of the cook. He wasn't well-liked, and they were glad to be rid of him. On Monday, the man bought a padlock for the freezer, and every day he sat with his wife before the fire on their pale-blue loveseat, looking into the flames, into the rain outside.

Meanwhile, in the freezer, their secret crusted over with frost, then snow, then finally, weeks later, with a thin layer of pure ice. Blue frost decorated his beard and formed lacy patterns in his hair. Sheets of ice webbed his fingers, crept under his fingernails, whitened his eyebrows, and covered his yellow teeth.

Finally, four weeks after the *problem*, as it had come to be called, the woman heard a voice. She was preparing for a charity planning dinner, and at first mistook it for the wheezing of her perfume atomizer. But, when she'd finished spraying herself, had leaned forward to inspect the wrinkles forming at the corners of her mouth, she heard it again.

Honey, she said, did you hear that? But her husband was in the shower, and couldn't have heard a thing. Besides, she wasn't sure what the voice had said, if it had said anything at all, or merely mumbled quietly in her ear, so instead she busied herself buttoning her blouse from the small of her back to the nape of her pale neck.

But that evening, the voice returned. They were in bed, and it was after midnight. Cold, the voice seemed to say, cold and dark in here. Honey, she said. Her husband's eyes were wide and glassy in the night. Did you hear that?

What? her husband said. But he sounded shaky and uncertain. In the silence that ensued, they heard the mysterious voice again. Actually it was more a chorus of very quiet, raspy voices, each complaining of the cold, the darkness, and the endless electric humming of the freezer. The dog, sleeping at the foot of their bed, did not stir.

It's the cook, the woman said.

Go to sleep, her husband told her. It's nothing. This is Foxhall Drive.

Eventually the strange noises ceased, but in her dreams, the cook rolled over in his icy bed, lifted the door, and dangled one frosty arm over its gleaming edge. The room seemed unusually cold, and when she awoke the next morning, she was surprised to see that she had twisted the covers around her toned body, and that despite it all, she was shivering.

Every night, they were tormented in this way, by myriad plaintive voices and premature frost on the windows. They tried extra blankets, earplugs, turning up the heat, even keeping the radio on into the night. But the voices continued, and the cold didn't seem

5

to originate from the room, but from within their very bones, freezing them from inside out.

When the visions started, they knew that something had to be done. The man woke in the dark hours of the morning to see a white thing, all frost and dry-ice smoke, wobbling in the bedroom doorway. Before he could nudge his wife, the frosty thing raised one oddly clenched hand, swept its snowy hair from its eyes, and moaned plaintively, filling the bedroom with a frigidity that neither of them had yet experienced, a cold so deep it stung.

Go away, the man hissed at the frosty thing. Shoo.

But the cook's ghost merely shifted its weight from foot to foot in the doorway and moaned. When it turned its head to look at the woman, she heard the dry cracking sound of ice giving in to the movement of its neck. Cold, the white thing said, dark.

Stop now, the woman said, who was not asleep, but who had been watching the thing through narrowed eyes since before her husband had even awakened.

The thing moaned, and stepped into the room.

Out, the woman said. Now.

Whatever it was did not seem to understand. It rocked from one foot to another, and stepped closer to the bed. Behind it were frosty footprints on the carpet.

The woman stealthily reached down to the side of the bed, and groped for her slipper. When she found it, she threw it underhand, in one deft movement, at the cook. But the slipper, spinning toe over heel, merely passed through the unhappy figure in the doorway, slapping against a marble urn in the hall.

You, the ghost said to the woman, and then, rippling, as if seen through water, it vanished.

From that day on, the man and woman did not get along as well as they had before the problem. Neither of them had had a good night's sleep in weeks, so they were grouchy to begin with. And, beyond this, the man found that the alabaster Pietà had sustained some damage after all, a thin chip to the heel of the left foot. And, though the woman maintained that it had always been there, she was nevertheless aggravated by the fact that the man took it as seriously as he did. Their room was now permanently frigid, and the woman's

6

left slipper, the one which had passed through the ghost in the doorway, was still icy to the touch.

The other servants had begun to talk among themselves, and they tiptoed gingerly through any room within earshot of the master or mistress. One of them is obviously having an affair, the upstairs maid was heard to have said, that's the only thing. But the gardener thought differently. It's him, he would say, meaning the husband. He's no longer . . . you know . . . things don't work for him. I know; I live right below them.

Whatever the reasons, the man and woman were not getting along, and already the thing had begun to venture beyond the grounds. Twice, the woman found that the lady across from her at the charity luncheon, where the Foxhall matrons planned their yearly events to help the less fortunate, was no lady at all, but the frosty thing, legs crossed, eating cookies. And, driving to work, her husband had often turned to look behind him, only to see the apparition seated, gazing wistfully out the window.

We are not people, the wife said one afternoon, who are bred to withstand discomfort. What we have to do, she told her husband, who sat shivering before the fire, is get the cook out of the freezer.

Her husband made a face. Couldn't we get someone else to do it, the maid, maybe? he said, though he knew that was not an option. His wife shook her head, exasperated. Already spring was sliding easily into summer, and pretty soon the kids would be home from Choate.

What we will do, she said, is let the cook help out with the Ladies' Charity Event.

Charity event, her husband said, looking into the hot fire.

It will be next weekend. We will all do our part.

Her husband nodded, waving his pudgy fingers before the fire.

They spent the next Friday night in the garage, carving the cook into manageable cuts, leaving them to thaw on top of the old white freezer. Although it was difficult work, the meat frozen and tough, by sunrise all was completed. There was more than either of them had ever expected, and, with the help of the new, unsuspecting, cook, a docile woman from somewhere south of the border, they spent the day over skillets in the kitchen.

All in all, they had to admit, the event that Sunday was a

success. The less fortunate came from wherever the less fortunate come from in droves. From beneath newspapers, from cardboard boxes, from park benches, the husband imagined. The community center was filled with their thin, alcoholic faces. They rummaged through the cast-off clothing, milled around by the water fountain, and most of all, ate the charity food, donated by the society ladies themselves, lightly seasoned with tarragon and bay leaves.

In the hallways, children played and ran among themselves in noisy crowds. Older girls giggled and sassed one another, while the boys, standing in groups of three and four, cast furtive glances in their direction. Even the most bedraggled of the adults stayed and ate full meals, joking noisily on the benches that lined the community center hallway.

If there is anything that warms the heart, the woman thought, standing in the throng of society matrons by the exit, it is helping those who are less fortunate. She sipped a glass of charity lemonade, looked out over the sad masses, and smiled serenely to herself. The other ladies in the charity organization were satisfied, too, nibbling sandwiches, eating cookies, chattering among themselves.

So things came to a happy conclusion. The husband and wife were no longer bothered by summer frosts, strange icy breaths on their backs, or sad voices mumbling in their ears. The woman could wear her favorite slippers once again, and the brass buttons of the man's blazer no longer stung his fingers with cold.

This is not to say that some things didn't change. Their new cook was caught sipping liquor from the cabinet and had to be let go. The chip to the left foot of the alabaster Pietà was declared beyond repair by their appraiser. It stands, to this day, damaged on the piano. And, most of all, the man and woman are haunted by a mysterious, glacier-like shift in neighborhoods, the occasional less-fortunate, drunken soul who wanders, out of place, beneath their bedroom windows. Sometimes they hear him complaining about his hunger, thirst, and in the wintertime, the unrelenting cold.

"—nobody knows what it
means, or how old it is."

THE ICE TREE
Catherine Berry

One of the few good intellectual pursuits of living in a small town is hanging around the local historians, especially when they're drunk. You know I love Tim, and I mean no disrespect. He's one of the sharpest men I've ever met; may I be as intelligent as he is when I'm whatever-the-hell age he is. Not only does he know his history, he's too smart to let a book have the last word, if his instincts tell him otherwise. He has a detective's stubborn passion for the pursuit of the truth—a necessary thing when you have to wade through volumes of dry record books, conflicting accounts, and the confused ramblings of elderly peers whose brains aren't nearly as well-tended as his. Like most homegrown intellectuals without the comforts of rank and prestige, he's tough as nails, passionately eloquent in his arguments, and about as no-nonsense as God made 'em. As a result, he likes fraternizing with eccentrics like me, primarily because I make him look good.

We hit his favorite bar now and then, one of those shabby-genteel affairs full of sepia-tinted war heroes memorialized over the clusters of bottles, John Deere hats, and old movie posters filling the corners, and a well-watered wall of spider plants hanging down in front of the window, keeping out the light and the noise from the street. Our meetings usually start out with chat about the latest happenings, with Tim filling me in on all the dirt and dish of our respectable townspeople. By the time he's on his fourth beer, however, we're past facts and delving into the soul of things. Tim calls it an old man's fancy, and maybe he's right, but secretly I suspect he needs an oddball brain like mine to blend with, someone to receive those notions that prey on his own, impossible to prove but difficult to dispel.

Tim probably doesn't remember that night in its entirety. It was a long session, listening to him, nearly three before I shook off my shock to make my good-bye and stagger home. Maybe he stayed to keep drinking, to get it out of his system. He will remember that he told me about the bones. It made the front page of the paper three weeks before, and they'd been milking it ever since. Not that there's much to tell. The electric company was putting down cable in a patch of ground, when one of their people found some suspicious shapes in the dirt. By the time they'd finished digging, there was a full set of bones, later revealed to be those of a woman.

No, I'm mistaken—not a full set. The fingers were missing. By this time, they'd reported the incident, and the police were out, shutting down the operations, and closing off the area. It took ten men, breaking up the soil across a mile-wide diameter of field over the course of a week, to find those little finger bones, as far and wide as they'd been strewn out. By this time, we were using phrases like "The Crime of the Century," and eagerly waiting for the reports of the forensics team called up from the city.

The experts examined the skeleton, and pronounced it to be over a century and a half old. Furthermore, they had found no signs of violent death, either by human or animal attack, which made the distance of the finger bones all the more bizarre. Even without scientific evidence, there was intense speculation that something horrific had happened in that field, back when the town was in its infancy, not much more than a few buildings and farms surrounded by prairie, some sadistic murder or cruel Indian ritual. As you can probably guess, all the local historians were running wild. Knowing Tim, he couldn't be bothered to give them the time of day; he loves his own opinions too much. Having heard everybody else's until I was on the verge of strangling the next idiot who brought it up, I was nonetheless glad to get his phone call inviting me out for a beer, knowing what I would be walking into.

"You ever hear of a 'weather witch'?" he asked me, as I settled down on the stool in front of a cold one. I was proud to say I had: my grandfather claimed he could take a Y-shaped tree limb, and use it as a conductor to bring on the rain clouds. Tim's eyes immediately rolled up to heaven, and he muttered that he wasn't surprised, with a family that had created me. I took a long gulp of beer to keep myself civil: sharp minds often breed sharp tongues, my mother used to say. "This town has a history of weather witches," he went on. "You still have the occasional old lady talk about mixing up soot and children's tears to bring on the rain. They used to advertise it in the paper, did you know? All the way up to the '40s. Editors eventually gave that up after the war, with the GI's and the new generations settling here.

12

Too backward. Too embarrassing."

I recalled last summer's drought. Some restless nights, with nothing but reruns on TV, I'd take my bicycle out for a few hours. Skimming along the country roads, sometimes I passed cornfields, and I'd see people standing among the tall, dry stalks, under moon glow in a cloudless sky, staring out to the horizon. At the time, I thought they were praying. I repeated this to Tim, and he nodded with a frowning smile, half impatience, half respect. "It's an old superstition. Hard to shake off."

"Maybe it works sometimes," I countered, thinking he meant the prayers.

"Maybe the rains just came, anyway," he snapped back.

I took another diplomatic gulp of beer, and reminded him that he was the one who'd brought up the subject of weather witches; and they might have been praying, and if so, we were in the wrong institution for discussing God. He chuckled at this. "When Jesus was in the Temple with the elders," I added, "I bet they all sounded like you."

"Thank you. Whatever. I was talking about weather witches," he continued dryly, "and the reason I mentioned it is, I'd gone back 150 years in the Courthouse archives—did a weekend in front of the microfiche—God! My eyes! I was looking for murders, massacres, disappearances, any kind of local hanky-panky..."

"Sounds pretty vague."

"No, I know how to weed out the usual town scandals of the time—they either started shooting or they didn't—pretty straight-forward. Anyway, anyway—that pasture where they found the bones—belonged to the Keltner family, roundabout 1840, sheep and cattle. They sold it in 1846, when it went barren. Years afterwards, nothing could grow there, not even weeds. This was right after a terrific cold snap. Months of icy weather, the worst in our history."

"What's that got to do with some corpse?"

Like most—hell, ALL—intellectuals, Tim could be charmed by the sound of his own words. As he talked, his eyes had softened, his hand on the bar twitching as if tempted to reach out and grasp what his mind's eye was forming. My comment had startled him, and then he smiled in the oddest way, as if relieved to be back to reality. "Have you ever heard of the Ice Tree?" he continued. "Wait—

course not—you're not a townie. They wouldn't mention it in any of the history books here, and you won't hear it from any historian, because it's too damned embarrassing.

"The legend's attached to the Keltner pasture, that one night it was hit by some…what do I want to call it? Some super-storm of ice, just as the cold snap ended, all in one night. In the middle of the pasture, there was said to be a tree that hadn't stood there the day before, a tree made entirely of ice. The next day, it just melted into the snow, and when spring came, that ground was dead underneath, and stayed that way for well on a hundred years. I heard this story when I was a kid. The so-called weather witches all remember it." Tim was drifting into reverie again, and I decided not to disturb him, though my mind was humming.

"So I told you about the weather witches, didn't I?" he snorted abruptly, and I nodded. He shook his head distractedly. "Trying to keep it all straight. Anyway, they used to advertise in the papers. This one in particular caught my eye." Retrieving it from his jacket pocket, he unfolded and passed me a blotchy microfiche copy of a newspaper page, with a boxed-in announcement in ornate letters:

NATURE REINED IN
A lady of Clarow County
Is pleased to offer her unique
WEATHER-GUIDING ABILITIES
To farmers in need.
Mrs. Jackson has plied this
RESPECTABLE TRADE
Through FOUR COUNTIES
With
Generally pleasing results.
VIOLENT WEATHER has been soothed,
And UNCOOPERATIVE WEATHER
Has been rendered generous.
Only God-fearing Christians need
Enquire. No ruffians, Indians or
Irish, please.

I slid it back. "Ohh-kay. What else you got?"

Tim called the bar lady over for another round. "The courthouse records gave her full name as Jane Jackson. I couldn't find evidence of a Mr. Jackson anywhere, so the 'Mrs.' may have been a front."

"To keep things respectable."

"Right. Not much else exists on Mrs. Jackson, excepting that ad. But as I'm sifting through the 1846 newspapers, I notice—right after the blizzard ended, and the Keltner's pasture has been sold, she just—what I mean is, the ad disappeared. I need to back up, here. She'd had this ad in the paper once a month over the course of the year. Then winter hit—storm of the century—and it was in the paper every week."

"So she could take care of ice and snow?"

"Apparently, she thought she could," he replied, taking up his next beer. "The roads are a menace, nothing but frozen mud for miles, people stranded in their homes, supplies can't come into town. I think somebody took her up on her offer."

"Any way to know who?"

His eyes were staring out to nowhere now, like those people in the field. "Of course, nobody would have recorded it. Especially in the aftermath. I'm betting it was the Keltners. It makes sense. They've got sheep and cattle, probably freezing to death in the barns—a more immediate crisis than those farmers with just crops to worry about. In fact, the farmers with corn and wheat and the like would be less concerned about a cold snap—might positively welcome it, to kill bugs."

"Tim? Sorry, man—you've lost me."

He inhaled sharply, tossed back the rest of his beer like a man taking medicine, blew out his cheeks, then turned to face me almost violently, leaning hard against the bar. "There's an old nursery rhyme—all the old folks learned it on the playground—nobody knows what it means, or how old it is." He paused, weaving a little on his stool. "Well, I know how old it is. It comes from the time of the Ice Tree. Someone made it up, and the kids passed it around like a boogieman legend, until the words lost all meaning, and then it was just something you chanted while jumping rope. But there it is, completely intact, truer than any official record. Poor Mrs. Jackson."

"Still not following you."

15

He stood up, a little unsteadily, and slowly raised his arms, fingers splayed. In the smoky background, a circle of drinkers darted a look his way, and the older ones among them grinned and nodded in recognition. "'Run right home on winter's day,'" he whispered, "'or you'll end up like Janie Jay/Stand stiff upright in the snow/With nowhere else on Earth to go.'"

Tim suddenly cocked his head my way, and I felt it all come together in my head with an unwanted clarity. In my imagination, I could see the Ice Tree for what it was, and it was now clear to me, when the ice melted and the land thawed, what must have slid into the mud, and been buried for a century and a half.

"'Slowly melting in the sun,'" Tim continued, in a gentle sing-song, "'Breaking off branches/One by one.'" The question of the scattered finger bones was now answered, as Tim slowly curled each one of his in, pinky to thumb. We stared at each other, stricken, isolated from the bar and the whole rest of the world by what we now knew. Poor Mrs. Jackson, indeed.

I struggle against the eclipse...

THE DREAM
Jo Gallagher

I hardly know him. What am I doing in bed with him? More importantly, what am I doing married to him?

A whirlwind courtship it is not. A man as cautious and methodical as Walter Neilson does not indulge himself in anything as mundane, as plebeian, as a meet-her-today-marry-her-tomorrow romance. No, his is a carefully planned, carefully executed thrust and parry: lunch here, dinner there, a regular procession of outings followed by long periods of absence. Keep her off guard. Let her wonder.

Wonder I do. When I eventually feel comfortable enough to request an explanation for such erratic dating, his reply comes easily.

"It's hard to see the forest for the trees. I need to back off every once in a while. Besides," Walt adds, "I'm afraid I'll move too fast and scare you off. I don't want to do that."

Eventually he proposes. I attempt a modicum of revenge. I keep him waiting more than a month for an answer, telling him I've given no thought to marriage.

Walt isn't handsome, not in a classical sense, but there is an enormous appeal in his thick dark hair and piercing gray eyes. A tall man with broad shoulders, he makes me feel petite and protected whenever we're together, though I, too, am fairly tall. Walt is intelligent, witty and well-read; we share common interests and never lack for conversation.

So, we are married. Instead of the quiet, almost-private ceremony I envision, we have a formal wedding with hundreds of guests. The elaborate reception at a local country club is followed by a quick honeymoon at a popular resort. A honeymoon made for lovers, it is all a woman could wish.

Here we are, barely two months later, nestled spoonlike under a heavy warm comforter. We've fallen asleep after a delightful evening of lovemaking that begins in the den and ends in our king-size brass bed.

Now I am awake. Abruptly. A dream-turned-nightmare leaves me shaking. My mind tosses feverishly while my body tenses against the slightest movement. Desperate not to waken the softly snoring

Walt, and still under the hypnosis of slumber, the tentacled hold of an unwelcome fear has me in its grip.

Fear of my husband.

The dream begins easily enough. Walt and I are making love, as we had actually been just a few hours before. In the afterglow, we bask in each other's arms, just as we had earlier. And, just as earlier, we drift off to sleep. Or I do. Walt is stroking the back of my neck, planting little kisses at the base of my hairline. I feel him gently tug me onto my back, trailing his kisses across my shoulder and up onto my face. The lovely thought that he wants me yet again is confirmed when he rises above me and straddles my body. I keep my eyes closed, savoring the lingering aroma of our earlier passion. I pretend sleep but my unruly mouth quirks a tiny grin in his direction.

He shifts his body, his knees pinioning my arms along my sides. My smile widens as I picture myself his "prisoner of love." Opening my eyes, I prepare to tease him about how insatiable are his lusty appetites. My words arrest at the feral gleam radiating from his pale eyes. The light of a nearly full moon shines through the window, illuminating his whole upper body. The shadows of the blinds make tiger stripes across his face and naked chest. A rapacious animal returns my startled stare as his lips curl back, revealing white and curiously pointed teeth.

"Hey, love," I begin, wanting to dispel the odd feeling creeping along my spine.

Just as I start to speak, Walt picks up his pillow. With both hands clutching it, he slowly and inexorably brings it downward, toward my face.

"Walt!" I scream.

The pillow stifles my protest. I turn my head, trying to avoid it. I kick and jostle, my hands useless against my body. I can't breathe. I can not breathe! Darkness crowds my mind, rapidly closing in from the edges of my consciousness. I struggle against the eclipse, against the burning in my lungs, against the weight of the pillow over my face. Just as I know this is the end, know I am dying . . .

I wake up.

A dream. Just a dream. That's what I keep telling myself as my heart decelerates and my ragged breathing returns to normal. I lie motionless, struggling to come to grips with the horror that has awakened me.

What do I really know about Walt, this almost-stranger I've married?

Incapable of anything else, I review what I do know: his family, his friends, his job, his religious beliefs, his ideals, his childhood, his goals. Again and again I parade it before me as I distance myself from the dream.

I grow calm. Eventually I even chide myself. How can I doubt this wonderful man? Finally, amusement sets in and I suddenly want to share this ridiculous experience with the man I love.

"Walt? Hey love, wake up." I shake him gently.

"What's the matter?" he mumbles, his voice laden with sleep.

"I had a really bad dream. Hold me?"

"Tell me about it," he says, as he shifts onto his back, pulling me into his arms.

I tell him the whole thing, including even the doubts I had. I keep repeating how awful the dream was: his being on top of me, pinning me down, the look in his eyes, the pillow coming down over my face.

Now as wide-awake as I, Walt laughs.

"You mean like this?"

Without warning, he rolls his body up and over me. He straddles me and presses my arms to my sides with his knees.

"Walt, no!" I protest, appalled that he wants to reenact the terrifying nightmare.

Just as in my dream, moonlight pours through the slatted blinds, bathing his torso with those hated stripes. With an all too real feeling of déjà vu, I look speechlessly into the face of a beast—a beast who is picking up a pillow and lowering it toward me. Hopelessness overwhelms me as the pillow closes over my face. The weight of it suffocates. Any will to struggle lies completely dormant within me.

This time I know I am going to die.

Then . . .

I wake up.

"Can't be too careful with our young ones."

SOON AND VERY SOON
Donna Volkenannt

She was the first person I saw when I walked in to the Veterans Hospital with my daughter and grandson. The woman's thin hair was styled in old-fashioned finger waves, yet the color was anything but old-fashioned. Her burgundy bangs were combed down over her pink scalp; wisps of sable framed the sides and back; silver dotted the temples and crown. She wore crimson sweatpants and a purple fleece top. Her gold lamé flats looked out of place on an icy day the week before Christmas in St. Louis.

When I glanced her way while searching for a place to sit, she smiled. I returned the smile, wondering if she looked in a mirror before she left home. The seats in the reception area were almost all taken, by veterans waiting for the bus to Jefferson Barracks. I spied one small space on the end of the couch, right next to her. I stepped over a half-dozen pairs of outstretched legs and wedged myself into the narrow corner, cradling my grandson in his bulky snowsuit while juggling my purse, a diaper bag, and a receiving blanket.

As soon as I sat down, the woman leaned forward, clutching a straw purse next to her chest, like a mother nursing a newborn child. She reeked of Emeraude, stale coffee, and cigarettes.

"Now, ain't he a precious one," she said, flipping back his cover. She coughed into a tissue several times, waking Emmett from his nap. "Pretty blue eyes, same as his blanket."

"Thanks." I turned him away from her, hoping he would fall back to sleep. "He just dozed off."

"Here, let me take that," and she snatched the diaper bag from my arm while I unzipped his snowsuit. "What's his name?"

When I said, "Emmett," the woman dropped the diaper bag on the floor.

"Praise God!" she said, raising her palms towards the ceiling, then lacing her fingers under her chin. "That was my son's name. Don't hear it much these days."

"He's named after my daughter's father-in-law." I nodded towards Megan who was waving at me before stepping into an elevator at the end of the hallway. "She's on her way to visit him in the ICU."

While I struggled to unbutton my coat, the woman said. "I haven't held a little one in so long. Mind if I hold him while you settle in?"

"He's pretty fussy," I answered, not wanting to hand my grandson over to a stranger, especially one with a cough. "And he has a cold. I wouldn't want you to catch it."

"I don't mind catching a cold." She pulled an inhaler out of her purse and squirted a dose into her mouth. "Already got lung cancer. Doctors give me three months, tops."

"I'm sorry," I said. "But, he's about to fall asleep."

She nodded and her eyes reddened. "That's OK," she said. "I understand. Can't be too careful with our young ones."

A few minutes later the woman said, "My name is Alma Fudge, and this here's Mr. Coleman Jackson." She tilted her head towards the large man, with skin the color of burnt toast, who sat across from us.

"I'm Nora," I said, not wanting to announce my full name to a room full of strangers.

Mr. Jackson tipped his dark blue pork pie hat and said, "Nice to make your acquaintance, Miss Nora."

"Mr. Jackson don't look sixty-eight, now does he?" Alma asked.

"No. He doesn't," I said.

He stared at his feet, obviously embarrassed by the compliment.

"No need to be modest," Alma said. "And wait till you hear what he did for a living."

"What'd you do?" I asked, not wanting to seem rude.

In a raspy voice, he said, "Got a job as a carpenter after my hitch in the army. Was in the carpenters' union for almost thirty years. My crew helped build the old arena."

"Our Lord and Savior, Jesus Christ, was a carpenter," Alma said. "That's a right-fine profession."

Mr. Jackson shrugged. "Thank you, Ma'am."

"My Harold was a hog farmer," she said, "till he took sick." She glanced at the clock above the information booth, then at the bank of elevators. "He should be here any minute."

She told us she was waiting for her husband to return from x-rays and get his prescriptions filled before they drove back to their home in southeastern Missouri.

"He's got diabetes," she said, leaning forward. "The doctors cut off his right leg a few years back. But the VA gave him one of them motorized wheelchair-scooters. It's almost as good as being able to walk. Maybe even better, Harold being so big and all."

Mr. Jackson said, "Just found out I got diabetes last month." He took off his hat and thumbed the brim. "Hope the doctor's don't cut off my leg."

"Now don't you worry none," Alma said, patting his hand. "Harold went years before they had to cut on him, and you're in better shape than he was at half your age."

Mr. Jackson sighed and kneaded his hat even faster.

A blast of cold air from the revolving door caused Emmett to wake up and begin crying. I stood and tried to rock him back to sleep. Each time he started to nod off, the door swung open and another gust filled the reception area, causing him to fuss. Alma tapped my knee. "That draft's not good for babies. Makes them colicky."

I wrapped Emmett tighter in his blanket and stuffed his pacifier in his mouth, but that didn't help. When he let out a piercing scream, a man with a black cap emblazoned with KOREAN VET adjusted his hearing aid, and several people in the reception area stared at me. I plucked a bottle from the diaper bag and walked away from the door until Emmett quieted down.

"There's only one thing worse than a colicky baby," Alma said when we returned.

I continued to rock him and stood with my back to the door.

"My Emmett was a colicky one, too. But he's dead now. Died a week before his twenty-first birthday. That's the only thing that could be worse."

"I'm so sorry," I said. I didn't know what else to say, and I hoped either Harold or Megan would return soon.

Alma pulled a tissue from her straw bag and dabbed her eyes. "Yes, sir. There's no hurt worse than losing your own flesh and blood. A young one shouldn't go before his parents."

"Amen!" Mr. Jackson said. He had a far-off look in his eyes. "My grandson was killed last year. He was only 18."

25

"Lord have mercy," Alma said, raising her eyes upwards. "What happened?"

Mr. Jackson bit his lip, then said, "Got shot standing on a street corner, minding his business. He was a good boy, never got into trouble. They just drove by and shot him. No reason at all. And the police still don't know who done it."

She leaned over and squeezed Mr. Jackson's shoulder. "Never know what the Good Lord has in mind for us. We just have to trust in His mercy."

Mr. Jackson nodded. "If you don't mind my asking, how'd your boy die, Ma'am?"

She removed her inhaler and took a deep breath. "He was sodomized," she said. "And them devils carved thirty-three crosses all over his body, same number as the age of Our Savior when he was crucified."

"Good God," Mr. Jackson said. He shook his head, then covered his mouth with a hand.

"That's horrible," I said. My knees buckled and I sat down. "I'm so sorry."

Alma rocked in her seat. Her voice sounded hollow, as if she had recited the litany of her son's torture a thousand times. "They burned him with cigarettes. Cut off his scrotum, and left him to die."

The conversations of passersby in the reception area stopped. A handful of people paused to listen. One snoring vet woke up at the mention of the boy's mutilation.

Alma's eyes glazed. "But he didn't die. Not right away, at least. He entered God's kingdom two days later in the hospital, surrounded by his family and friends."

Mr. Jackson leaned forward in his chair; his hands rested on his knees. "They ever find out who killed him?"

Alma closed her eyes and shook her head. "Never did. Emmett must've knowed them, but he never did say. He was such a brave boy, and gentle, too. A month before he passed on I found him kneeling in the mud next to the hog trough. 'Momma,' he told me, 'I wished I was dead.' I think Satan heard him and sent his minions to hurt my boy. Such a sad soul," she said. "He was big, like his daddy. And shy. He never dated a girl. Not even once."

She dug into her purse, pulled out a square of tissue wrapped with blue ribbon, and unfolded it like a treasure map. "Here he is," she said, removing a pair of yellowed photographs. "This here's the only picture of him I have. He hated to have his picture taken. Said it took away his soul."

She handed the photo of her son to Mr. Jackson, who passed it on to me.

"It's a copy of his driver's license. My daughter in Kansas City has the original one. In color."

"Nice looking," I said, staring at the picture of a sad-looking young man with a pumpkin face and raisin eyes.

Using her sleeve, Alma wiped off the second photo before handing it to me. It was a Polaroid of a headstone etched with: OUR DEAREST SON, BORN APRIL 18, 1971. DIED, APRIL 10, 1992.

"That's a lovely headstone," I said.

"Genuine marble. Imported all the way from Italy. Took five years to pay for it. Saved up my tip money. I was a cosmetologist," she said, plumping up her curls. "Had my own shop in the basement before Harold got diabetes. He's a gospel singer now. Even recorded a tape. 'The Old Rugged Cross' was his best song. He even sang it on the radio once."

"That's one of my favorites," Mr. Jackson said, passing the photo back to Alma.

"After one fella heard Harold on the radio, he drove all the way from Illinois and bought hisself a tape. Paid fifteen dollars cash money and didn't even blink." Alma took one last look at the photos before bundling them up.

"That's a fair price," Mr. Jackson said. "Wouldn't mind having one of them tapes myself."

Alma took a paper and pen out of her purse and scribbled a note. "Here's our address and phone number," she said, handing the paper to Mr. Jackson. "Come visit us any time. Next year, in the springtime, I know Harold will welcome the company. And bring your fishing pole."

"I just might do that," Mr. Jackson said.

Alma clasped her hands. "Oh, and there's a Missionary Baptist church in town. One where all the black folks go. The pastor there prayed Psalm 23 for Emmett at the funeral home. And his wife dropped off a homemade sweet potato pie at the house after the

27

service. Everybody said it was the best pie they ever ate."

Mr. Jackson licked his lips. "Ain't nothing tastes better than homemade sweet potato pie."

Emmett started fussing again. When I stood up, I spotted Megan stepping off the elevator. She walked behind a man in a motorized scooter.

"Here comes my Harold right now," Alma said, waving at a huge man wearing bib overalls and a John Deere cap. "Maybe I can get him to sing for us."

"That would be nice," Mr. Jackson said.

When Alma asked Harold to sing, he didn't need any encouragement. As soon as she mentioned "The Old Rugged Cross," he sat up straight in his scooter, blew his nose, and cleared his throat.

Megan gave me a curious glance while she zipped up Emmett's snowsuit and wrapped him in his blanket.

"I'll tell you in the car," I whispered, just as Harold began to sing.

His voice was like water from an artesian well—deep, rich, and clear. Everyone in the lobby stopped to listen.

When he finished with, "*I will cling to the old rugged cross and exchange it some day for a crown,*" Mr. Jackson and I applauded. Megan's eyes welled with tears.

The man at the reception desk announced, "The shuttle bus will leave for Jefferson Barracks in ten minutes."

While the other veterans hurried out the door towards the bus in the parking lot, Mr. Jackson chatted with Harold about fishing lures and sweet potato pie.

Megan handed me Emmett while she loaded up the diaper bag.

"Mind if I have one last peek at that grandbaby?" Alma said.

"Would you like to hold him?" I asked.

Alma reached out, then cradled my grandson in her arms. She rubbed a finger against his cheek and cooed, "There, there, little one," then kissed his forehead before giving him back to me.

"Thank you," she said. She brushed a tear from her cheek, then turned towards Harold, who had put on his scarf and was buttoning his coat.

On his way out the door, Mr. Jackson said, "I'll be sure and call before I stop by."

Harold nodded, then pulled his cap down. He turned to Alma and said, "Ready, Mother?"

Alma nodded. She looped her purse over her arm and trailed behind her husband with her hand on his shoulder. "How about 'Soon and Very Soon'?" she said.

Thick snowflakes began to fall as Harold and Alma paraded out the door into the brisk December afternoon singing, *"Soon and very soon, we are going to see the King."*

And like a memory of something
I couldn't fully grasp, I felt a chill.

CRYSTAL JUNK
   Matt Bird-Meyer

A junkie turned blue in my bathroom today.

I suppose I liked him. Maybe I even considered him a friend. His name was Alex and he spread himself very thin, yo-yoing from the city to the suburbs and deeper into the small towns where innocence and conservatism masks an affluent drug culture. Drugs flow in and out of these little towns like wastewater. It was perfect for Alex because of two things. One, he couldn't sit still for more than a minute. Two, he had to make a living and all of the kids were buying.

Alex rarely came around and when he did, I rarely saw him. I mean he was there all right, but he was always busy fussing with something in foil, something in tiny boxes, or he paced and talked and it was like he wasn't there at all.

Alex made fun of me for calling him a junkie.

"It's crystal. We're not junkies," he said. "Besides, it's only recreation. It's just an occasional thing."

That's why every ten minutes I could hear the rasp of a lighter in my back room. Alex was out of sight, out of mind most of the time.

I don't know why he turned blue. I think he talked too much and he finally ran out of wind, like he sort of self-suffocated alone in my bathroom. Recreational drug users don't overdose, right?

He is gone now and it is quiet in my house. But his eyes seem to linger and his hair, the stringy, frayed mess on his head, remains as much as those eyes. Even when he wasn't talking, those eyes told stories. Alex's stories blended into a constellation of other stories, of fighting with cops in an alley, chasing thieves away from his apartment and locating components to make drugs.

Alex taught me how to cook crystal meth. He appeared at my house one morning and needed a place to stay. It was his last visit.

I learned that the process of making crystal is simple, in theory. It's all about the colors, like panels on a flag—red, black and white: red phosphorus, black iodine and white ephedrine.

There's red phosphorus in the gritty strike pads on matchbooks. There's black iodine in horse pills, the stuff for the hooves. Then there's the blessed ephedrine, ephedra in its pure form, or *ma huang*, derived from an Asiatic shrub.

Alex visually demonstrated each step of the process with his arms, hands and entire body. The jewelry he wore tinkled all over with every movement. The bracelets chimed on his wrists, the rings clanked on his fingers and the shiny silver bulldog medallion clunked on his chest like a heartbeat.

I didn't want to listen at first, and his rapid discourse made him hard to follow. But I soon found myself straining to piece together every word, every sentence. It was like a delicious puzzle, something naughty that the school hood tells you after school in the parking lot. Alex rubbed his nose, the rings clicked and he laced into the story of his business.

"There's a shitload of ways to peel away the undesirables and glob out the tasty stuff," Alex said. "Most of the time, you gotta pull out the ephedrine from ordinary gas station uppers. Sometimes you can find some chump pushing pure ephedra."

Lots of drugs, mostly allergy medicines and diet pills like Metabolife, use ephedrine as a key component, but in our time of blue junkies it's not as readily available.

"Druggists pull it off the shelves in the bigger cities, and leave it to the goodness of the community in the small towns, confident folks can keep an eye on the sale of the product," Alex said.

Their myopia was Alex's payday. He fed off communities like these, conservative on the front end and hideously desperate and broken on the back end. Usually, these were places with at least one convenience store owned by a Middle Eastern family who were more than willing to sell boxes of unlikely products that, when stripped down, become components to an intoxicating brew.

He said the drug companies do their best to discourage meth dealers. "They insert wax or create something less desirable like pseudoephedrine. The government imposes import-export and domestic thresholds on shit like benzyl cyanide, toluene and methylamine. The sale of ephedrine is always monitored. That's why it's best to grab it out of an existing product." He sounded like an underground chemistry teacher.

Alex knew he was preaching to the uninitiated and he was confident. He was a magician revealing the secrets to his tricks, like a father passing down the family's secret recipe. Maybe he knew his end was near.

"I have goals, you know," Alex said. "I have high goals, aspirations, I guess. You know, I can work. I can do whatever, jump from job to job. This is it, you know, this is it."

Usually, these high goals resulted in bad batches, the dirty drugs even a dead man would turn from.

Alex assured me that he tried his best to cook his stuff clean. It was always the other fools who were in a hurry, spilling things, staining their hands with the red phosphorus and using contaminated utensils and glassware. And typically, there were three guys to cook a batch. Each one was responsible for one ingredient.

"But there's this new kid from a small town east of the city who started showing up at the Fast Stop I discovered," Alex said, his eyes wide. "And he cleans out all the boxes of matches before I can get there."

Alex paused. He didn't move, just stared forward.

"This kid won't last long," he said.

Alex shook his nappy head a little and trotted over to my front window and peeked out at the street. The magnesium street lamp winked out as if to take a break. I watched the square patch of pale light on the carpet disappear. Alex stood at the window until the lamp kicked back on, turning his face a whitish blue.

"You'll need acetone at some point," Alex said. "Just before it all comes together and forms a column of poisonous gas."

That's when the magic globule appears, wrapped like a present in corrosive ooze.

Nerve damage, damaged dopamine cells, scarred lungs, heart damage, bleeding brains—the happy consequences of prolonged exposure. Alex coughed into his fist a lot.

The magic globule is frozen and later dried. It becomes, first, a magnificent display of crystal webs and finally, when dried, a very lucrative powder.

"It's funny, you know," Alex explained. "This powder draws all the evil in society into one ball of angst and tweak. You wouldn't believe what some people do to get it."

"*You* are a tweaker!" I said, probably too loudly. "You tweak and all of your friends are tweakers. Right?"

He stopped, briefly, both hands clasped together.

"Why, that's a very good summary, my friend," he confided.

Then he quickly sat in my recliner and immediately jumped back up. He skipped into my kitchen and pulled out a frozen pizza from my freezer without asking. In two swift actions, he stripped the frozen pizza from the box and ripped it out of its plastic wrapper. He spun the dial on the oven and flung it onto the top rack to cook.

He talked the whole time, and I kept listening. I realized that I was listening to a completely different story. He talked about music, or was it some movie he watched? I stopped caring and decided to try something. Instead of trying to follow his story, I replayed some fond memory, something like making lunch or reading a few more pages just before the sun set. It worked just fine.

When I looked up he was standing over me, looking at me.

"Sorry, what'd you say?"

"Nothing."

Then he ate my food and slumped onto the couch, thumbed through a magazine, tore out pages without asking, cut out images, letters and eyes and pasted them onto a piece of cardboard I was saving to make postcards.

I woke up in the middle of the night to pee. As I walked back to bed, he came through the front door. Still half asleep, I couldn't figure out what was going on. Then I realized he hadn't slept at all. Rows of magazine collages were lined up along the entertainment center like panels to a surreal painting. There was Madonna's head pasted on a scarecrow, buttons lining her mouth. There was George Clinton peering back at me with fish eyes while two slugs made love on his chest.

I found Alex in the bathroom that morning. A prism that hung from the window cast two rainbow trapezoids on his closed eyelids. The only thing I could think was that he sure needed some sleep.

I don't know why he turned blue. Maybe his tongue swelled and he suffocated like a dog.

I'm only glad I found his body and not him choking on a

swollen tongue.

He looked like a junkie to me, all blue and propped against my bathtub on an elbow. Even blue and contorted, Alex still looked like he was posing, showing off the bracelets on one wrist and the chains that hung around his stiff neck.

The light from the prism drifted from his eyes, across the bridge of his nose and disappeared into the hair on the side of his head. I walked out of the bathroom and into my living room, where dozens of magazine eyes pasted to cardboard squares stared at me.

Alex's story of the magic crystal now seemed like a horror-laden fairy tale. Its toxicity was certainly evident. I know it made Alex feel like hell. He never slept. And as I walked around the house, I noticed how deep his mania went. He rearranged the frozen items in my freezer and took inventory on a little slip of paper. Alex arranged all the CDs in the rack by year, alphabetized the movies stacked on another rack and rifled through my file cabinet.

I remember one evening, I told him I'd never tried crystal and he kept flicking his lighter. His eyes seemed to change color, his irises swapped hues and his hair hissed and seethed, splitting apart at the ends. A fly landed on his arm and I noticed his shoulders, how they seemed composed entirely of thin collarbones stuck in sharp, pointed shoulder blades.

It was pretty awkward trying to explain to the cops why there was a dead, blue tweaker in my bathroom. I told them Alex must have died from natural causes.

"No, I don't know why he turned blue," I said.

That night, I sat reading in my living room. I put my book down and thought for a second that maybe I missed Alex. Then again, there really wasn't much to miss. I sipped coffee. The room was quiet, there were no voices; nothing called me. And like a memory of something I couldn't fully grasp, I felt a chill. No windows were open. Yet a noticeable breeze cooled my legs propped on the ottoman.

There was a hum and a sort of a tick. Ah, the ceiling fan, of course.

I thought of Alex's face, distorted, blue and dead. He had died. He walked into my bathroom to do what? To sleep? To get high? To die? Wasn't the first rule of drug dealing to never do what you sell? I wanted to ask him about that and wished he were sitting by me so he could tell that story. Then again, what the hell was I thinking?

Maybe he was trapped in my bathtub forever. Maybe I would have to cook a good batch of the magic crystal in the tub to release his damned soul.

To me, he was like a fast car driven hard. He had a body just like me and everyone else, one he relied upon dearly to get through life. But like a fast car, Alex sped up, slowed down, sped up even higher and down even lower until he was abandoned in a heap, forgotten and left to rot.

All the good times, all the steep hills it had to climb, the cold starts, the cruising on fumes to the nearest station, all the times it came through for him were thrown into the passing breeze like a whimper.

You hear the cries all over and think they're meaningless, because they sound like false stories. Alex spoke to pass the time. Alex talked like he was running out of time.

He liked to think he told stories with hidden meanings, that he could abuse and insult all his enemies with never-ending rants. I imagined he talked to keep himself company as he leaned against my bathtub on one elbow, cool and fulminated like a stationary lightning bolt.

His funeral was delayed almost one week. It seems the county couldn't find his mother or any other family member. I heard they finally found her passed out somewhere in Texas.

At the service, I looked around at all the people who came to see Alex's body one last time. Two guys sat alone in the back pew. They had dark eyes, gold and silver chains and nice shoes. They twitched a lot and coughed, sometimes in unison. Their pockets twittered every few minutes and one at a time they would disappear to the back of the church and mutter into a cell phone.

Alex's mother sat in the front row, sobbing and shaking. Her eyes looked bruised and baggy. She rubbed her nose and sniffed like a run-down clock. In the far corner, rows of candles flickered and danced. Statues stared down as if sick from the height. Alex lay in a black box off to the right of the altar; blue splotches showed through the thick skin-tone makeup applied to his face and hands.

A priest spoke at the dais but I couldn't understand what he was saying. At times I could make out a few forced rhymes, but he mostly tailed together a never-ending string of words. His hands danced in circles over his head and crossed in front of him as if cutting down thin stalks of wheat. The glare of rosy-colored sun stained his cheeks.

The middle rows of pews were dotted with young kids wearing concert T-shirts, ripped jeans, bed hair and ponytails. Others wore nice thick-knit sweaters, turtleneck shirts and nice hair. Alex's mother appeared to be the only adult in the room, besides the priest.

As soon as the priest uttered his "Amen," the kids scurried away in different directions. No one seemed to want to stand around and talk. I sat near the back of the church, just a few feet from the two guys in the back pew. I wanted to talk to them, but as people filed out I lost them in the crowd.

I had to sprint to catch up to them just before they reached an old El Camino in the parking lot. One kid smirked and asked me what I needed as the other reached into a deep pocket in his cargo pants. I told them I just wanted to talk and they looked at each other and looked around. They said they had to go and didn't have time to talk. I pulled out my cigarettes and a matchbook. As I struck the match, they stared, not at me or my cigarette, but at my matchbook.

The kid on the right pulled his hand out of his pocket and reached up to pick at his ear. I noticed that his whole hand was stained red.

"Where do you live?" asked the other kid.

They traded turns coughing.

"Huh?"

"Where ya from?"

I told him I lived in the city and he nodded, uninterested.

"So, whaddya wanna know?"

"Nothing," I said. "I think I know too much as it is."

He tapped his friend on the shoulder and both jumped into the car, and chugged off in a cloud of acrid smoke.

Even the pauses gave her no rest, for they
were but warnings of what was to come.

RAYMOND'S BEAUTIFUL SMILE
Judith Kelvin Miller

Click, scrape, sproing, pause.

Click, scrape, sproing, pause.

Myra's fists clenched and unclenched in rhythmic pulses of annoyance, her nails creating half moons in her palms. She cringed more intensely with the clicks than with the scrapes and sproings.

"Mmrmph, whas mirmph oss?" Raymond asked as he emerged from the master bathroom to stand before her in all his glory— middle age lapping over the waistband of his striped boxer shorts, graying black chest hairs pushing through the threadbare tatters of his athletic shirt.

Every time he stood in front of her like this, skinny walrus tusks of floss hanging from his mouth, Myra would marvel. How could a man who was such a futz about his personal hygiene and inner-body health—they should have bought stock in Metamucil—be such a slob on the outside. He refused to let her throw out any of his underwear until it was well beyond even the rag stage. And the detritus of the flossing? All over the house! Her back ached from stooping and bending to retrieve little threads from the oddest places.

Bad enough he would try to talk while flossing, letting the string drape on his lips and down his chin like petrified drool as he stood barking orders or criticizing her defect of the day. Bad enough the leftovers escaped to all corners of the house.

Even worse were the obstreperous noises!

Myra had a problem with sharp staccato sounds. Her pet peeve, recorded in her high school yearbook: people who crack their knuckles. Merely reading the phrase sent shivers up her spine.

The sounds of Raymond's overindulgence in the art of dental hygiene were, at first, a little pet peeve. In fact, in the early, innocent days of their marriage she was intrigued by his fortitude. He never missed the healthful morning ritual, even before the subject of flossing had become a fire and brimstone topic from the pulpits of hygienists.

Jane Hargrove embraced the techniques of that trade with a passion. Like all in her profession Myra had met, Dr. Overbie's hygienist was a young thing with a petite body, tiny palms masking the strength of a pro wrestler. Gums sore, jaw aching, Myra felt like the loser in a boxing match after each visit. And like a misbehaving grammar school pupil. Another part of the hygienists' code to which Hygienist Hargrove adhered was the requisite scolding of one's victims with the tenacity of a pit bull, the righteousness of a nun. Myra wished she could forgo the lecture as well as the pain.

Not Raymond. He worshipped Little Miss Janey and the gifts of knowledge she bestowed upon him, despite his Ph.D. in flossing.

Yes, Raymond was flossing before flossing was cool, he being a devotee of anything so obviously beneficial. Or was Raymond a devotee of anything everyone else thought futzy—that he could follow rigidly and lecture about to the rest of the world? The distinction between "adherent of the beneficial" and "futz" had blurred in Myra's mind long ago.

After a few trips to Harlot Hargrove, Raymond expanded his repertoire. The morning ritual became a many-times-per-day event. It began to slurp over into their lives away from the house. On those rare occasions when they ate out, usually at someone else's expense, he would pop into the men's room just before dessert in order to remove any offending bits and pieces. This was especially likely to happen if he had been eating roast beef. But wasn't he always eating roast beef?

That time when he had returned to the dinner table at the Reynolds' house with floss stuck to his suit collar had sent Myra to a new level of disgust.

But none of that behavior had the impact of the noises she heard in her own home. The clicks and scrapes and sproings were prime examples of her pet peeve. Even the pauses gave her no rest, for they were but the warnings of what was to come.

"Pet peeve" did not evolve slowly into "major annoyance." It burst out of its shell of minor avoidable bother to become inescapable torture. That cataclysmic event had occurred one rainy evening in October, five long years ago. Myra knew the length of time precisely. Yesterday CeCe had been declared cancer free.

Myra and CeCe had been best friends since childhood,

remaining in, in Raymond's too-often spoken words, "constant contact." On only one point did they disagree—choice of mate. Myra thought CeCe could have done better than Frank. CeCe thought the same about Myra settling for Raymond, beginning her assault just one week after Raymond first asked Myra out.

"But that smile, CeCe. Those beautiful teeth. I cannot resist a man with such a gorgeous smile—with teeth of such whiteness. It shows he thinks highly of himself to take such good care of himself. And someone who takes good care of himself can't help but take good care of those he loves. Yes," she had continued in a wistful manner, "Raymond has a beautiful smile."

CeCe was not won over, but on that day, back in the late '60s, decided to hold her tongue, not say, "Love is blind."

CeCe's resolve did not last long. She took up the attack shortly after Raymond and Myra married, was still on the aggressive on that fateful day five years ago when she called and asked Myra how the old fussbudget was doing. Myra had laughed and asked CeCe what was new with her and her old stick-in-the-mud. There had been a long silence, a silence that told Myra something was wrong.

"He's not throwing you out is he?"

CeCe's problem had had nothing to do with her relationship with Frank—only with herself. A lump had been discovered during her last check-up. The lab results had just come back. The diagnosis was definite—breast cancer.

Myra took a turn at remaining silent. Following that brief pause she began to do what friends are meant to do—offer her moral support and any practical support CeCe could think of.

It was while she had been on the phone learning from CeCe the horrid diagnosis, while she was deep in the midst of this most critical of phone calls, emotionally drained from her friend's tragedy, that Raymond catapulted Myra's pet peeve into a full-blown intolerable flaw.

Raymond sat himself down on the edge of the bed beside her and began to floss as only Raymond could floss. The "click, snap, sproing" grated on her already stretched nerves. Something inside *her* clicked, snapped, and sproinged.

Fortunately, it also paused.

Always before that day, Myra had surreptitiously managed to

avoid hearing the sounds that so unnerved her. Whenever Raymond would begin a session of his avocation, Myra would simply leave the room.

Raymond never seemed to notice.

But on that occasion, when Myra was so deeply involved with her friend's plight that she had no thoughts of leaving the room, could not have because she and Raymond had no portable phone, would not have because how could one say, "Hold that thought that your dying, CeCe, while I get the other phone"—on that occasion Raymond had begun the click-scrape-sproing ceremony practically right at her ear. The insult upon her important conversation more than peeved Myra. It enraged her. But she remained calm, just waving Raymond away with an expression of annoyance.

Raymond noticed.

For a while after that call, Raymond made a big show of leaving her earshot before flossing, as if he were some cavalier gentleman not wishing to offend his lady. His feigned consideration lasted a short time. Less than a month later Myra began getting the impression he had begun to make sure she *was* in earshot before he flossed. Although he didn't go so far as to awaken her if she were sleeping, he did seem to be following her when she tried escaping.

Five years she endured assault upon her sensitive senses.

But those were five years of limited intrusion. Only on weekends did she have to tolerate the sounds more than twice a day. That was about to change. In just a few short weeks Raymond would turn 65. Retirement loomed before him, and before Myra.

Myra didn't know how she'd cope with him and those obnoxious jolting sounds on an unrelenting, continuous schedule.

"Mmrmph, whas mirmph oss?" Raymond asked again, this time in a *louder* unintelligible voice, jolting Myra from her reverie.

"What, Raymond, I can't understand you?" Myra asked with exaggerated pleasantness.

Raymond paused, not removing the floss from his mouth, to enunciate with great exaggeration, "Myra, where's more floss? We out? This is the last piece."

"Don't worry. I have one cached away. I'll go get it."

"Thanks. Be sure to pick some up soon. Having only one left

isn't a good safety net."

"Yes, Raymond."

"When you're buying more, see if there's any new kind. You know me, always the adventurer."

Indeed he was. Without her glasses on, Myra couldn't tell the color of the dental floss hanging from each side of his mouth, but she knew. She'd been picking up the disgusting minty-green strings for a week. Before the green, there'd been the turquoise interwoven with white. Before that—you name it, he'd tried it.

"I'll be sure to check." She smiled a gritted-toothed smile.

"Oh, stop and pick up a car headlight. One's burnt out."

"Sure, Raymond."

Myra walked the drugstore's familiar dental hygiene aisle, stopping precisely at the right section. The dental floss display was, she thought, like a house on an old milk wagon horse's route—a location to which she returned so repeatedly it had become embedded permanently in her memory pathways. Thought was unnecessary to tell her she had the correct location.

"And what splendid array you are in this morning," she told the containers hanging before her. Ribbons, strings, waxed, unwaxed, woven, mint, cinnamon, giant size, travel size.

As per Raymond's instructions, she carefully checked for new entries in the battle against the dual enemies of tooth decay and gingivitis. She chose several enticing flavors of a new brand, "Sweet Tooth Dental Floss" and walked to the front of the store.

Glancing at the newspapers displayed near the checkout counter, Myra's eyes were drawn to a headline. She selected that paper and read avidly, until her turn came, then tossed the newspaper onto the belt with the many packages of floss.

The cashier gave first the floss, then Myra, a quizzical look, commenting, "Sounds disgusting to me. I like candy, but not for flossing. Yech." She paused suddenly, realizing remarks about a customer's selections were inappropriate. "Sorry. Each to his own."

Myra laughed reassuringly. "Don't worry. I agree. They're for my husband. He loves flossing—can't go more than a few hours without it. Still has all his permanent teeth, so there must be something to it. He also likes variety. I'll see what he thinks of these."

"Guess it's better than booze," the cashier remarked, handing Myra the change.

All during this inane, everyday occurrence, two items had been dancing around in Myra's head, weaving around each other, timidly at first, like two people fated to be joined, slowly approaching closer and closer until they found themselves inexorably intertwined.

"Don't ya' think?"

"What? Oh, sorry. You're right. It's much healthier." Myra put her change in her purse, then left for the auto parts store to get the headlight and another item she had suddenly decided to add to her list.

Myra bent over the garage workbench, worrying, reminding herself she'd never been good at crafts, or anything requiring delicate manipulations. "I have gross fine-motor skills," she joked to herself, then remembered the many times she'd said that line in response to Raymond's chastisement of her almost-illegible signature as he looked over her shoulder while she was writing checks.

"But there's a way when there's a will," she reassured herself, encouraging herself with a memory of Stephen in his scarecrow costume for the second grade's rendition of *The Wizard of Oz*. Instead of risking a disaster by attempting to sew, she'd gotten a gunnysack from the grocery store and carefully wound pieces of yellow yarn in just the right places. It was a rather grand costume and garnered her many compliments. Best of all, Stephen had loved it.

Dear Stephen and lovely Lucille. How she wished she could see more of her children—and grandchildren. But Raymond was of the opinion that once you've raised them and launched them you've done your duty. "Seeing them once a year at Christmas is all you need. I never knew my grandparents and look how well I turned out." How often he had said that; how often Myra had wished she could see her children and grandchildren more; how often she wished her grand-children knew her as more than just a voice on the phone or someone to whom to write thank you notes.

She returned her focus to the job at hand. She definitely had the will to find a way.

* * *

44

"Hey, Myra," Raymond yelled pleasantly from the bathroom, then emerged, as always, to stand before her, floss dangling. "This stuff really tastes great. I may start flossing twice as much, now that I'm retired and have all the time in the world."

"You do that Raymond. Nothing would please me more."

"I know it's kind of soon to ask, Mom, but have you thought about what you might do."

"Oh, yes, Stephen. I have been thinking. I think I'll move to Denver."

"Mom, that would be great! Stephen and I would love to have you be part of our families. We always wanted the kids to know their grandparents."

Myra hugged her daughter, and squeezed the hand of her son. Her three grandchildren stood around her, not yet fully comfortable with this woman who had been practically a stranger for most of their young lives.

She thought for a moment of the bright, warm future, surrounded by her family, then thought for a moment of the last few months.

A calendar appeared in Myra's head, some days highlighted.

Day One was the Awakening, the day she had gathered her tools—the newspaper article that had guided her to her new life; the Sweet Tooth Dental Floss; and the other sweet item, the liquid of great significance in that article, the liquid she'd bought at the auto store.

Day Two was the Preparation, the day when she'd bent over the workbench in the garage, carefully unwinding and dipping and rewinding, calling upon a will that let her find the way to overcome her natural clumsiness.

Day Three was the Planning, the day she'd figured how to time things to coincide with the last week before CeCe's husband Frank retired. Myra knew he would not want to complicate his last days as County Coroner.

Day the Last, the day when she knew Raymond would no longer click, snap, and sproing.

But all his faithful devotion had paid off for, as he lay before them all, no one could deny that Raymond had a beautiful smile.

45

It was oafish; any idiot could scare a child.

OL' MAR AND THE WEREWOLF
Tim Hammack

Thwarted by his talk about wolves, Bivinr slipped away from Ol' Mar's group and sought out Molligo. He found the boy with his two friends, Mousling and the Trug, Dego. They were eating their rations in silence.

"Any of you gikkechs hear that wolf howl?" Bivinr barked, exploding from the trees.

"Yeah," Molligo answered pleasantly. "It was pretty loud, wasn't it?"

Bivinr squatted and lowered his voice considerably. "You believe that bechido the Dakkers are spreading about werewolves living in these woods?"

"Don't know about that," Molligo confessed, "but I'd say it's kind of spooky. There's a wolf pack following us, eating our garbage, you know."

"Yeah," Bivinr agreed. "Ol' Mar saw 'em on guard duty the other night. They're just wolves, though, right? Ain't no werewolves out there?"

"I don't believe in werewolves," Molligo confided. "The chaplain said the Good Book doesn't mention them anywhere. Dumdum sure believes in them though. He says the werewolves rob people during the night."

"Yeah, I heard," Bivinr fretted.

"Mine grandfather, he wuz werewulk," Dego announced through his thick accent.

"Really?" Molligo's eyes widened. Dego rarely spoke, and when he did Molligo tried to encourage more of it.

"Your granddad was a werewolf?" Bivinr asked nervously.

"Yah," Dego answered as though he was talking about the weather.

Bivinr waited for Dego to flesh out this terrifying revelation. The hairs on his neck pricked. The moonless evening closed in around him. One minute passed and then another went by without Dego providing elaboration. Bivinr growled, "'Yah' what? What do you mean he was a werewolf?"

"Uh…" Dego rued opening his mouth. He could never think of anything witty to say, and when he did it lost itself in translation. Now he had gone and made an inside joke about his family to strangers. He envied Bivinr's snappy wit, and for a second he had thought a story about his grandfather might win him some popularity. His nerve vanished though as the spotlight shined in his eyes. Dego recanted, "I don't know. People say too much about my grandfather."

"Oh," Bivinr retorted, confused. Were werewolves not prowling about hunting for flesh, he would have let Dego have it. Bivinr grimaced. If Ol' Mar and the gang were to see him confessing his fears to Molligo, Mousling, and Dego, they would rib him to pieces. Bivinr realized he just needed to keep his cool and act like a man. Even roly-poly Molligo did not believe in werewolves. Bivinr hawked a wad of phlegm, spat, and tramped away without further ado.

"Hey, Bivvich," Bodzodo cheered. "You got back just in time. Ol' Mar's telling us about the time he killed a werewolf!"

"Really?" Bivinr was surprised. "Ol' Mar, you seen a werewolf?"

"Damn right! The no-good sack of bechido was raiding my daddy's chicken coops!"

"Your chicken coops?" Bivinr questioned. "Aren't werewolves supposed to eat people?"

"Not this gikkecher," Ol' Mar quipped.

"Are you kidding, Biv?" Yag laughed. "Where Ol' Mar comes from, it's the people who eat the werewolves!"

"Damn straight!" Ol' Mar stuck out his chest. "This was about twenty years ago when I wuz a young gikkech like Bivinr there. My daddy comes bustin' into my tool shed where I wuz fixin' my grammy a new rocker. He's raging like a hornet on fire, and he says, 'You goddamned son of a goat, one of your gikkeching, sack-of-bechido hounds done got in and thrashed my coops.'

"'What?' I says to my pa, 'them hounds wouldn't do no such thing. Them's boar hounds and they can't be bothered with no sissy hens.'

"'Well, goddamn it,' my daddy replies. 'I got me a thrashed coop, and all I see is them goddamn mutts of yours idlin' around lickin' their mangy chops.'

"'Hell, no,' I tell my pa. 'Them's good hounds. I tell you, it's a goddamn coyote or one of them gikkeching wolves come out of the forest.'

"'Okay, you son of a bitch,' my pa answers. 'I'll believe it when you show me the goddamned carcass!'

"'You got a deal, pa!' I tells him, and me and my daddy shakes hands on it.

"A couple of weeks later, my daddy and me bring home some new hens. I set up a roost in the trees above the coops thinkin' to catch this mongrel next time he strikes. He don't come the first night, and he don't come the second night, but on the third night, just as I'm fixin' to drift off to sleep, I hear somethin' snapping twigs in the woods. I fetch my shotgun out and starts hunkering down to get a good shot at whatever comes stumbling out of them bushes.

"I wait and wait; the noise gets closer and closer. Luckily, there's a full moon out and I can see pretty good, because what comes out of them bushes was darker than the devil's armpits. I sees this big, hairy thing come leaping out of them bushes, and when I say big I mean it must've been bigger than a bear, but there ain't no bear, I reckon, that could've jumped like that varmint did. That thing tore straight for my daddy's coops, and I let rip both barrels at it. I hear a scream like no scream that ever came from no wolf, and see the thing fall dead in its tracks. I scramble down to take a look at it, and I'll be a goddamned son-of-a-bitch if what I found wasn't the largest gikkeching wolf ever to bechido on God's green earth. The no-good cocksucker must've weighed at least one thousand pounds and was the size of four men. Ain't never seen no wolf with such dark black hair before, neither. I run to fetch my pa from bed figurin' he'd be mighty pleased.

"When I drag my old man out there, he takes one look and swears, 'Turzo Sokos! Riz, I think you gone and killed the devil herself!'

"My daddy wants to fetch the priest to look it over, so we drag the bitch into the tool shed. Goddamned, if that work didn't nearly break our backs! After that, I locked the shed real good and tight and tuckered in bed for a couple hours shut-eye. At first light, my daddy and me bust that shed open to see exactly what it is I bagged. I tell

49

you—holy goddamned son-of-a-mother-gikkeching-whore! What we find lyin' there was a man as bare as the day he was born.

"My daddy sends me to fetch the priest, and I come running back about noontime. The priest takes one look at the body and starts trembling and chanting from his prayer books. He tells me I done killed one of the devil's seventy-seven sons and wants me to go live at the church for a week and bathe everyday in holy water. I tell the priest I don't believe in no god or no devil, but my daddy smacks me upside the head and makes me do it anyhow. That's the end of the story; I don't reckon the devil's too sore at me 'cuz I never saw hide nor hair of her other seventy-six sons."

"Holy bechido!" Bivinr gasped with eyes popping out of his head. "You're not hooding us—are you, Ol' Mar? That really happened?"

"Ye, sir," Ol' Mar solemnly vowed. "It happened just like I told it."

Corporal Dembeho spat, "Ol' Mar, if that's not the most stinking pile of bechido I've ever smelled!"

"What?" Ol' Mar cackled. "You calling Ol' Mar a liar?"

"No," Dembeho clarified. "I'm calling you a dumb-ass! Whoever heard of the devil having seventy-seven children, one of which busts hen houses? You would think that a son of the devil would aim a little higher! Ol' Mar, you're feeding us a load of bull."

"I'm telling you what I saw with my own hands and killed with my own hands!"

Yag and Bodzodo had a good laugh at Ol' Mar's expense, but Bivinr shuddered. He edged a little closer to the dancing fire. A wolf shrieked somewhere out in the darkness.

The days passed, and the caravan marched on. One night Dumdum, the Tarukei cook, harvested a stash of monkshood and tainted several pounds of jerky. Before dark, he sowed the poisoned bait throughout the camp. The captain caught him in the act and put a fast stop to his foolishness. Dumdum reacted by stringing the rest of the monkshood around his neck, wrists, and ankles.

Despite his superstitions, Dumdum had purportedly converted to the faith. Molligo felt an obligation to look out for him.

The Corporal had assigned Molligo, Dego, and Bodzodo to

escort the cook while he hunted mint leaves in the forest. Dumdum normally approached his work with absolute focus and sobriety. This evening, though, he fluttered about nervously, glancing over his shoulder every few minutes. "Mr. Dumdum, what's worrying you?" Molligo asked.

"Watch for wolf man," the cook muttered, using what little Leitonese he knew. "Is wolf man country."

"Dumdum, what do you mean 'wolf man country'?" Bodzodo did not deny that the werewolf stories spooked him at night, but daylight rendered them absolutely absurd. He worried that Dumdum was losing his mind. Dumdum cooked too well for the boys to let him lose his mind.

"Is werewolf home. Is watch day, attack night."

"What do you mean, 'watch day, attack night'?" Bodzodo demanded. He carried his rifle slung over his shoulder, and with his free right hand he gripped Dumdum's shoulder.

"Wolf man follows in day, attacks when sleep." Dumdum stared into Bodzodo's eyes, begging for recognition.

Suddenly, a branch snapped. The sound came from the slope above them.

The cook blanched. "Wolf man!" he gasped.

Bodzodo grabbed him with both hands, "What do you mean? What are you talking about?"

"Wolf man! Wolf man watching! There!" Dumdum pointed up the slope at a clump of trees.

"Bechido!" Bodzodo cursed. He unslung his rifle. The sun still shined brightly, and if something really was watching them from the top of the hill he needed to get to the bottom of it now. He growled and charged the hill.

"Wait, don't go alone!" Molligo gasped. "C'mon, Dedro!" Molligo chased after Bodzodo.

Dego blinked his eyes. He looked at Dumdum, and Dumdum looked back at him. He realized that not a great deal was going on at the bottom of the slope with Dumdum. He sprinted after his comrades.

When Molligo reached the top, he found Bodzodo scratching his head and looking around.

"I don't see nothing," Bodzodo complained. "Dumdum's going

nuts."

"I bet he saw a deer," Molligo groaned.

"You idiot!" Saryomeer slapped his little brother so hard that the boy's wolf mantle swiveled sideways.

"I'm sorry, elder brother!" Sarturlaa sniveled and rubbed his cheek.

"If you keep screwing up like that," Saryomeer hissed, "the boss is going to make me send you home to Ma. He thinks you're just a kid, but I swore you could hack it. Now, you're making me look like a man who's not good for his word!"

"I'm sorry, elder brother," Sarturlaa whimpered. "I didn't see the branch, my mask—"

"Shut up!" Saryomeer gnashed. "The boss doesn't want to hear excuses! Now straighten your mantle. We'll lay low until it's clear and then go back to stalking the foreign devils."

The two boys hunkered close to the ground. After Sarturlaa had snapped the tree limb, Saryomeer had grabbed his little brother and fled for cover. They dived into a gully and scrambled beneath a dead tree just as they heard the Leitonese soldiers reach the top of the slope.

The boys had been tracking the foreigners for three days. Their boss was planning something big; he wanted to sack a Leitonese caravan. By day, Saryomeer and Sarturlaa trailed the Leitonese; by night they returned to their boss to report. The boss said he was happy. The Leitonese were walking into his trap.

Saryomeer's boss, Baaryobaar, "Big Baar," had earned a reputation for himself as an innovator and a self-starter, a head above his peers. Fate drove most bandits to their profession. For example, an honest army captain might resort to brigandage to provision his men. A simple farmer might turn to crime after years of drought had threatened to destroy his family.

Baar regarded such pragmatic ventures as unimaginative and perpetrated in poor taste. In Baar's view, a bandit was more than a man (or a woman—Baar had never met a woman bandit but figured she would cut quite an image) who mugged people; a bandit was a professional. As a professional, a proper bandit owed clients something in exchange for their goods. In Baar's case, he gave them

52

entertainment.

Baar had not stumbled upon the bandit's path by accident. He and his brother, Sul, had formed their gang with a strategy in mind. The idea had formed during Baar and Sul's childhood. An old, bitter hermit lived in the woods near their village. The villagers had many bad encounters with him. He was quarrelsome and territorial. He believed the entire forest belonged to him. A rumor started that claimed the old man could transform into a black bear at night. Baar and Sul found that hard to believe. They decided to sneak into the woods and see for themselves.

After much creeping about, they stumbled over the hermit's cabin, but the old man was away. Baar and Sul broke into the shack and found a huge fur coat hanging on the wall. The coat had been crafted from a bear's pelt with the head still attached. Sul discovered that he could pull the bear's head over his own and wear it like a mask. This gave Baar an idea. He proposed they hide out and pay the old hermit back for all his mischief. The boys hid in the bushes near the cabin and waited. When the man returned, the boys sprang howling from the bushes. The old man's heart could not bear the fright, and he collapsed dead. This left Sul and Baar the sole inheritors of his bearish secret.

Sul thought it would be fun to play up the hermit's ruse and see if they could expand his legend. Sul began stalking around in the bear suit after dusk, while Baar began spreading new tales about the old hermit. His grandest yarn purported that the old warlock was summoning an army of demons to destroy the town, wandering around at night recruiting soldiers in his bear shape. This straw broke the camel's back, and the villagers stormed the forest. Baar and Sul watched the old man's cabin burn to the ground with their precious bear suit.

Four months later, the town experienced its worst winter in five generations. Starving wolves poured into their peaceful valley. The animals were as tall as men and covered in thick, black fur. Their breath steamed in the cold air like the scalding vapor of a hot spring geyser. Their eyes burned like the embers of a smoldering cooking fire. People could not believe that the winter had blown the wolves in; they feared that the old hermit was exacting his revenge. Word spread that the wolves could dress themselves in human skins and masquerade as people. During the day, they disguised themselves as townsfolk and walked among the villagers.

Baar and Sul believed none of these tales. After all, they had invented them for laughs. Baar concocted the story about the wolves wearing human skins. This had set Sul thinking. Wolves wearing human skins reminded him of that old man's bear suit. He dearly missed it and hated himself for letting it burn up in the shack. He thought it would be grand to make a new one. With the wolves at large, though, he figured he ought to sew a wolf costume instead. Sul's musings brought a devilish smile to Baar's face.

That night, the boys broke into the tanner's shop and stole two wolf pelts. They smuggled the skins to their cousin who ran a leather shop in the next town. They persuaded him to fashion two suits for them.

Two weeks later, the boys had their disguises. They could not wait a moment to put their new playthings into action. As soon as the sun went down, lycanthropy took over. Wandering in the forest that first night, they caught a villager coming home late. The werewolves sprang on him from the bushes. This sent the poor man screaming back up the path he had come down. The next day, Baar and Sul's first victim told everybody in the village about his terrifying experience. Sul and Baar sat back and let the rumors fly. The boys continued playing their jokes. They learned that frightened people were prone to dropping what they carried in their hands. They dropped such things as coin purses and expensive swords. Before long, the boys discovered that their little game was netting them an income.

The boys thought their bliss could never end. One night, however, a determined traveler turned the tables on them. Instead of fleeing, he smashed a club over Sul's head and batted Baar in the groin. The blow clobbered Baar, but Sul bounced to his feet and sacked the man. They wrestled until Sul wrenched control of the weapon. Too shaken to realize what he was doing, Sul pounded the man's skull to mush.

The boys crawled home. They pledged to freeze their operations and never touch the wolf costumes again. For the next several weeks they argued frequently. Sul wanted to abandon the sport entirely, but Baar, his strength returning, could not bear to part with the income it generated. He argued that the solution lay not in quitting the gig but in improving their fighting odds. He proposed that they bring a third hand into the partnership. He suggested a boyhood friend who was down on his luck. Sul resisted but soon gave up. With the third partner, the "Wolf Man Gang" was born.

The gang expanded to ten members within two years. Baar asserted himself as the gang's leader; Sul handled training. About this time, Baar began worrying that the gang was losing its style. It no longer handled its capers with the grace and the charisma of the early days. People regarded the Wolf Man Gang as a band of thugs. They thought the gang wore wolf pelts because it could not afford better clothing. Something had to be done. Baar decided that the gang needed to develop "pizzazz," something flashy that would restore its reputation. "Pizzazz" became Baar's mantra.

Baar tried many experiments. His favorite scheme involved abandoning the werewolf image completely. For a short time, the Wolf Man Gang transformed into the "Invisible Bandits." Baar envisioned his gang robbing clients (his preferred term) blind while they slept, arriving and departing without a trace. The idea sounded terrific, but in practice Sul found his brother's plan difficult to implement. Too often the boys tripped over clients in the dark or spent hours trying to unbuckle somebody's boot. An amorous sleeper once rolled over and embraced Sul while he fumbled with the man's diamond-studded belt. Kissed and told sweet things, Sul pulled the plug on his brother's pizzazz.

Baar refused to give up on pizzazz. Sul complained that Baar needed a magician, not a bandit gang, to make his crazy ideas work. This set Baar thinking. He wondered where he could get his hands on several hundred pounds of firecrackers.

The plan sounded fantastic. Picture this: The client and his party tramp through the forest. They feel happy without a trouble in the world. Suddenly, "wham, bam, bang!" explosions go off all around, and the Wolf Man Gang strikes like a hammer. Before the client even knows what befell him, the gang disappears back into the smoke. The client tells people he was attacked by wizards.

The boys loved the idea, even Sul. Everybody loved fireworks. Firecrackers were so colorful and flashy. Any plan that involved explosives was bound to succeed. During their first run, flying sparks set the boys' coats ablaze. This culminated with one lad charging into the clients' midst crying, "Put me out! Put me out!"

Baar experimented with a few more gimmicks, but the gang had lost patience with pizzazz. One boy quit and threatened to take the gang's secrets to the authorities. Rather than pay the ransom he wanted, Baar ordered his assassination. The depths they had fallen to drove Baar into depression.

The brothers began quarrelling again. Baar wanted to disband the gang and become a cabbage farmer. Sul countered that Baar's gimmicks were the problem and he was responsible for their predicament. Sul wanted the old days back. He wished he had never heard the word "pizzazz." Baar retorted that "pizzazz" was the band's only hope. Without it, the Wolf Man Gang was simply a rabble of clueless thugs.

After much shouting, insulting, and not speaking at all, the brothers reached a compromise. Baar proposed that the gang break the cycle and enter a new age of banditry. They would divide into two teams for each caper. Sul's team would handle the thuggery while Baar's team would arrange a sideshow to amuse the women and children. Baar did not like scaring women and children. It was oafish; any idiot could scare a child.

The concept proved a smashing success.

Baar discovered that he had a natural talent for being a master of ceremonies. He recruited two jugglers and a dwarf to accompany his performances. The women loved it. They were mostly servants or concubines and did not mind being entertained while Sul roughed up their insufferable lords. In addition, the women considered Baar handsome (though many complained he was too skinny in the chest), and adored his smooth talking.

The gang's appeal spread beyond women. To Sul's astonishment, soldiers became great fans. The Tarukei Royal Army never paid its soldiers, but it draped their commanders in riches. Soldiers enjoyed fewer rights than servants and spent most of their time performing the tasks nobody else would do. Baar made them laugh, and they did not object to him taking their warlords' money. Most begged Baar to take them as well. With already too many mouths to feed, Baar and Sul skimmed the best and sent the rest on their way.

As news about the quality of their entertainment spread,

fashionable people began seeking them out. The bored and posh found it novel to be held up in the woods by a traveling circus. Baar hired the best actors and opera stars. He recruited the cleverest magicians and the most beautiful singers. The mugging business receded. He kept it around as a trademark. Instead of charging admission, he began his performances with a mock holdup during which his pelt-clad employees walked through the audience "robbing" the ticket cost. Baar and Sul became rich men.

The Leitonese invasion changed everything. Businesses collapsed. Fortunes fell. Wealthy men found it difficult to put bread on their table. The forest filled with remnants of the Tarukei Royal Army's shattered forces. These soldiers reorganized themselves as bandits of the worst order. They harassed Baar's clients and even fought with his gang.

Morale fell to pieces. One after the other, the professional entertainers quit. His men defected to rival gangs. His treasury shrank smaller and smaller. Baar could do nothing to stop this. He flew into a rage. The Leitonese had brought all these troubles on him. Now he wanted revenge. He decided to sack a Leitonese Imperial Army caravan.

"Are you crazy?" Sul cried.

"You're damn right, I'm crazy!" Baar howled back. Those who still remained with them loved the idea. They had feared the gang was growing too soft. Baar offered them the chance for a comeback.

Dedro Dego yawned. He hated pulling guard duty during the last four hours of the night. He simply could not stay awake at that time. His head would start bobbing up and down like an ocean buoy, and he would drift in and out of consciousness. Inevitably, he hallucinated. He saw all kinds of things. He traveled to every place imaginable. He would find himself wandering through a maze of sleepy delusions and whispers. Demons played tricks on his mind; angels lured him to false paradises. Locked in this struggle, Dego felt little sympathy for his sleeping partner, Mousling.

Dego spied Mousling fast asleep with his back pressed against a tree. Dego gnashed his teeth.

"Hey, Bemizhi! Hey, wake up!" He grabbed the boy's shoulder and shook him vigorously.

"Wha...!" Mousling shrieked. "Wha...! Wha...!" He flailed his arms, panting in short, raspy gasps. He knocked Dego on the nose, and Dego kicked him in the shin. Mousling always fell asleep on guard duty, and he always flipped out when Dego waked him. Dego kicked him again.

"Wake up!" Dego snarled. "Wake up, Bemizhi!"

"Wha... wha..." Mousling repeated, growing calmer. He shook his head, figured out where he was, and muttered something. Dego wanted to kick him again but gave up on it. As he walked away, the familiar whine of Mousling snoring broke through the chorus of wolves howling in the distance.

Dego sat down. Guard duty never ended. Mousling sleeping on the job never ended. Nothing ever ended. He buried his face in his arms. Soon, he was running through a purple jungle chased by a band of headhunters.

The natives finished him off, and death jolted him awake. He smacked his gums and looked around. Two beast-like phantoms were hovering over Mousling. Dego groaned. Before long, he was a horse galloping across the plains accompanied by a talking dog who had the voice of his father. Dego hated late-night guard duty.

Sarturlaa crept slowly towards Mousling. He had never seen a foreigner up close before. The pale-skinned ghostie was snoring with its back propped against a tree. The ghosties were said to be giants, but this one was smaller than he was. He frowned, and wondered how these dwarfs managed to make such trouble. Sarturlaa noted that the creature was sleeping with its mouth wide open. He shook his head with disgust, and marveled at how stupid its race must be.

His older brother elbowed him sharply and indicated he should draw his dagger. Sarturlaa drew his knife slowly. Big Baar had instructed them to cut the sentries' throats. The ghostie looked so ridiculous, though, that he thought he would give it a little spook first. He straightened his wolf mantle, threw back his shoulders, and howled.

"Wha...! Wha...! Wha...!" Mousling gasped, shrieking.

"You idiot!" Saryomeer screamed at his little brother. He whipped his knife from its scabbard and charged the shouting guard.

Mousling's voice failed. He threw his arms in front of his face.

This swung his rifle, which he still gripped, out like a pike. Saryomeer collided with the blade and bounced backwards.

Mousling screamed with shock, dropped the rifle, and ran for the hills.

The racket jolted Dego to his senses. He heard men shouting from everywhere. Shadowy figures poured from the forest into the camp. The scene sent Dego's head spinning. His legs picked him up, his arms dragged him down, and on all fours Dego scampered into the dense foliage of the woods.

"Bechido!" Corporal Dembeho shrieked. "We're under attack! Circle! Circle!"

Mando Bivinr threw off his sleeping blanket and ripped his bayonet from its hiding place.

"Circle! Circle!" Corporal Dembeho's voice rose higher and higher. The Corporal's team circled back-to-back with their bayonets pointing outward. It was a drill they practiced endlessly but had never been called upon to use.

A long second lingered as the team poised at the ready. Their chests heaved and their shoulders trembled though the summer night was warm. Bivinr, who stood shoulder-to-shoulder with the Corporal, realized that shadows were racing towards him. The Corporal, a veteran of the war in Trugordia, howled a war cry and lunged forward. Bivinr heard what sounded like a bag of sand striking concrete, and an unrecognized voice yelped with pain.

Bivinr's turn came next. Something raced straight at him; it was howling. Bivinr's hands locked around his rifle grip. His fingertips dug into the wood. His toes dug into the earth. He remembered Corporal Dembeho's maneuver. He sucked in his breath. He closed his eyes. He jabbed the rifle forward.

The bayonet hit something very solid. Bivinr staggered back-wards, and then threw whatever it was over his shoulder. It was very heavy, and its momentum yanked him off balance. He fell on top of it, and his face hit a soft pelt of fur. The Corporal was shouting something at him. He pushed himself off the soft, sticky carpet and struggled to his feet. He jerked his rifle, but the bayonet would not dislodge from the dying thing. He yanked and he yanked. The Corporal shouted louder, barking orders at him that he could not

59

comprehend. He tugged again at the bayonet, but it would not come free. Shouts and cries bombarded him from every direction. Finally, he abandoned the weapon and spun around. He clenched his fists and assumed his best brawling stance. Poised there, he stood tight and trembling until shouts of "Stand down!" broke the tension. The Corporal barked, "Roll call! Roll call!" and the crisis officially ended.

Everybody answered the Corporal except for Dego, Mousling, and Ol' Mar. Molligo, his voice choked with tears, reminded the Corporal that Dego and Mousling had been on guard duty. He wanted to go look for them, but the Corporal forbade anybody from leaving.

"Where's Ol' Mar?" the Corporal demanded. Everybody looked at each other. No one could answer him.

"Stand still, you gikkeching son-of-a-bitch . . ." Ol' Mar muttered from the forest foliage; with the battle still raging, he aimed his rifle at a large fellow who seemed to be directing the attack . . .

When the partisans struck, Ol' Mar was urinating in the woods. He had heard what sounded like an army running and had ducked into the bushes. Within seconds, shadows streaked past him. He drew his hunting knife. It was sharper and stronger than the flimsy bayonet the army had issued him. He crouched low, savoring the pounding of his pulse. The camp's alarm rang out. Men were shouting. The forest was moving. He bit his lips and felt twenty-years-old again.

Ol' Mar knew the art of ambush. He had run quite a racket in his day. Experience told him to expect one or two more stragglers, and then he could safely strike back. Ol' Mar pounced when his gut told him to. He wrapped his arm around a neck, exposed its flesh, and slashed it with a single stroke. The victim stumbled forward, gurgling, and then collapsed. Ol' Mar beamed. Time had not robbed him of his touch.

Ol' Mar inspected the corpse and noted that the bandit wore a wolf mantle. He wondered what the story behind that was. He snickered and moved on.

He slinked to the edge of the camp and observed the chaos. Wolf-headed bandits were running everywhere. Ol' Mar figured he could fire blindly and hit something, but he saw no fun in that. He crouched, squinted, and searched for something shootable. The shapes were difficult to discern in the darkness, but he knew what to look for and quickly found his target. A big fellow was standing back shouting commands.

Ol' Mar relaxed and took up a comfortable posture. He steadied himself. He inhaled very slowly. The bullet departed at its own leisure. His target, Sul, went down. Ol' Mar grinned.

Sul did not need a bullet to tell him he was finished. Things had fallen apart the moment they were about to come together. The Leitonese had reacted too quickly. The alarms had gone up and sucked the gang into battle. He was a bandit, not a soldier, but here he was conducting war like a general, sending a rabble against professionals. So much was on his mind that he forgot about his brother. Maybe his brother had forgotten him, too. Death hit Sul from behind, and the moment passed beyond his concern.

Ol' Mar fired into the tumult as rapidly as he could reload. Pow! Pow! Pow!

Captain Breva restored order and assembled his men. They stood haggard but strong in the early morning calm. He tallied their reports and learned that the caravan had suffered only three injuries. This pleased him immensely. He wanted to recognize the brave man who had sounded the alarm that saved so many lives. Without giving imposters an opportunity to steal the credit, Corporal Dembeho rushed Mousling to the front of the platoon, and Sergeant Boroja giddily dragged him to the front of the formation.

The Sergeant saluted the Captain and proudly shouted his name and platoon designation. He relished the luck that had landed the deed in his hands. He did not know how Mousling had managed it, and he was not going to ask. Mousling was staring off into space, drooling, but a sharp poke brought the boy around.

The Captain laid a firm hand on the boy's shoulder. He turned Mousling around to face the men and gave his formation a short speech about duty, dedication, and diligence. He reached into his pocket and produced a medal. Solemnly, he pinned it to Mousling's breast.

Ol' Mar watched, and a wolfish sneer spread across his face. His sharp incisors flashed through the split between his jaws. Hearing the

Captain's words, he scratched his chin defiantly. The long, itchy fur had grown unshaven for several days, and his raking claws brought no relief. He shook his head, and his ears rang with the exertion. "Mousling..." he growled. He wanted to howl.

"Now I've told somebody, I feel better."

C. J. Winters

The old lady in the wheelchair peered up at me from filmed blue eyes. "I need to tell somebody something," she said. "You got time?"

I set down the vase of peonies I'd brought Aunt Maureen, asleep in the other bed, and pulled a chair close to her roommate. "I have until my aunt wakes up from her nap. My name is Carolyn. What's yours?"

"Nina. But everybody in the family called me Sissie. Doesn't matter, they've all gone on."

"I'm sorry."

She brushed my trite consolation aside like an annoying fly. "You ever see a ghost?"

Whatever revelation I might've expected, this wasn't it. "No, have you?"

Sissie's hands, the dark blue veins standing in high relief, trembled in her lap. "I reckon. Don't know what else it could've been. I was afraid to tell my folks. They were real religious and I figured they'd take me to the preacher and have him roast my feet in a bonfire till I said I'd storied." She chuckled, a dry, raspy sound that held little mirth. "You know the funny notions little kids get in their heads."

"Yes, I know. What is it you want to tell me?"

"I was five, I know, because it was the summer before I started to school. It was real hot, even at night, and if you listened close, you could hear the corn growing . . . little pop-pop sounds it made. Folks who never lived on a farm don't believe that. Anyway, one night it was too hot to sleep, so I knelt down by the open window and leaned on the sill and looked out at the stars. Then I saw something move, down by the old dry well. I couldn't see it clearly, but it looked like a lady. She was waving to me, like I ought to come down there."

I sneaked a look at Aunt Maureen. She was still asleep, her mouth open like a gasping fish.

Sissie continued. "Well, since the lady seemed to think it was important for me to come out where she was, I crept downstairs so's

65

I wouldn't wake anybody, and went out to the well. Sure enough, it was a lady in a long, whitish dress. Except that she and her dress looked kind of thin. You know, like the bandages they use on wounds?"

"Yes, gauze." By now I was intrigued and hoped my aunt wouldn't wake up before Sissie finished her story. "What happened then?"

"The lady acted real excited. She kept pointing at the well, and then she'd do this." Sissie folded her arms and swung them back and forth. "Like a little girl rocking her doll."

"And?" I prompted.

"Well, I was only five years old! What did she expect, anyway? But when she finally saw I didn't understand, she beckoned to me, like this, and I followed her. All the way down to our back pasture." She shook her head and sucked on her teeth. "If my folks had found out, they'd have skinned me alive! Sometimes I think my daddy *liked* using the razor strop."

I waited while her train of thought returned to its rails.

"Somewhere out in the pasture the lady stopped and pointed to the ground. I was afraid of our big black Angus bull, but he didn't pay us any mind. I remember I just looked back and forth between her and the bull. Then she made this kind of shoveling motion, like I ought to dig right there where she pointed."

"And did you?"

"Well, first I had to run back to the porch and get a hand spade. I was too little to use the big spade like my daddy. All the time I was gone the lady just stood there in the pasture, waiting, and that big old black bull, he just went on chewing his cud like there wasn't nobody within a mile. I dug and dug. That ground was *so* hard on account of we hadn't had any rain in who knows when. Then I saw something white sticking up in the bottom of the hole, and I started digging as fast as I could. It turned out to be a long, skinny bone. Well, I was real disappointed, figuring it belonged to some animal that died a long time ago. But the lady got all excited again, and she pointed back at the house . . . except when we got back there, I realized she'd been pointing at the well, not the house."

"Was it an open well? Or did it have a cover?"

"Oh, it had a cover all right, a big, thick piece of cement. I couldn't have moved it no matter how hard I tried. But the lady kept pointing at it, and then at the bone I'd brought back from the pasture. It seemed so *important* to her that I hung onto it, and the next Saturday we went to town, I wrapped it up in the blanket I carried sometimes, like it was my doll, and took it along."

Sissie paused as though reaching back eighty years in memory. I waited for her return, and Aunt Maureen slept on.

At last, she resumed her tale. "I took the bone, still wrapped in my blanket, to the doctor's office. I don't remember his name, but his office was in one of those pretty turrets that overlooked the square. I told his nurse I had a problem and I needed to see him."

She chuckled. "Imagine a little kid getting by with that today. Anyway, I showed the doctor the bone I'd found. To say the least, he was startled. He asked where I got it, and I lied. I told him I dug it up next to our old well."

"Then what happened?"

"When we got home, some men were digging all around the outside of the well. Of course they told my daddy what I'd shown the doctor. Seems the doctor told the sheriff it was the shin bone of a child, and they were looking for more bones."

"Did they find any?"

"'Course not! That's not where I found it."

"Then what?"

Sissie's scornful glance suggested I was being deliberately obtuse. "I walked up, bold as brass, to one of the men and said they ought to look inside the well. And they did. They even dug into the dirt in the bottom of it, where they found the skeleton of a little kid. My mama fainted, and my daddy looked like he wanted to. There was lots of excitement. The men thought the skeleton had been there a long time."

Forgetting about my aunt, I demanded, "Did they find out who the child was?"

Sissie shook her head. "The doctor said it was a boy, about my age. He was mighty puzzled, though, about the bone I'd taken him. He said it belonged to an older child, ten or twelve years old." Drained and weary, she sat back in her chair.

I said gently, "Is that all you wanted to tell me?"

Her head drooped forward in assent. "I always felt bad because

I never told the truth about where I found that leg bone. I was afraid of what my folks would do if they found out I'd gone outside at night and done what the lady told me to." She looked up, her ancient gaze still penetrating. "Now I've told somebody, I feel better."

"The older child might have been buried ages ago. Maybe it was an early settler, or an Indian."

"Maybe."

"You don't think your..."

"No!"

How did she know what was in my mind?

Aunt Maureen was still asleep, snoring lightly, and my own family was expecting me home to prepare dinner. I rose, then bent down and kissed Sissie on her dry, cool forehead. "Thank you for telling me," I said. "It'll be all right now."

Lost in her own long-ago world, it was as though she hadn't heard me. I turned and left.

On my way out, I stopped at the nurses' station. "My aunt is still napping," I said, "so I'll come back tomorrow. I was talking to her roommate, Sissie."

"Sissie?"

"Her real name is Nina."

For a moment a puzzled frown marred the young nurse's brow. "Nina . . . Oh, I'm afraid you're mistaken. Nina Freeman *was* your aunt's roommate. She died yesterday."

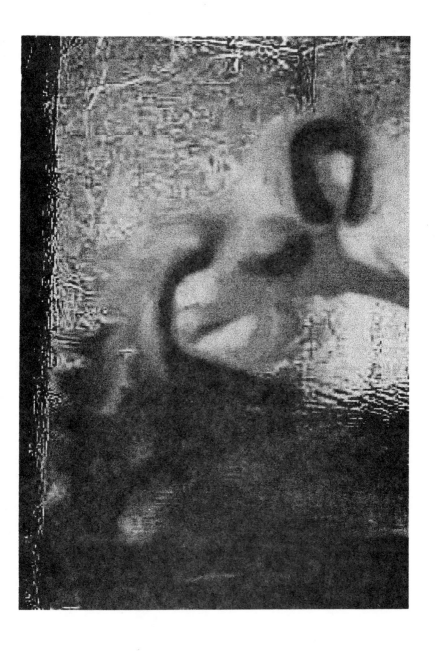

A couple of times that night we heard
sounds that sounded human, but not
really human, if you know what I mean.

MISS DELION AND THE BOOGER OF ROTTEN BOTTOM
Perry Beam

Back in thirty-three, I was out of work as a sheriff's deputy, fired by the new sheriff to whom I had taken a serious disliking from the moment we met. He was a nasty individual with no manners, brutish feelings, and very little upstairs. His existence gave rise to the phrase "big, dumb, and ugly," and he was referred to by his peers, in the five years he attended school, as "shit-for-brains." On Halloween in '05 he ran out of privies to topple so he pulled over his own and an hour later his horse fell in it and had to be put down. The year after he was asked to leave school, he chopped a hole in the roof of a house looking for buried treasure in the attic. When his father came in from the fields and saw him standing on the roof with an axe, he locked him up in the chicken coop for the night. It was the first good night's sleep anyone had gotten in years. He was definitely the kind of child that caused people to say, "That boy's not right."

I would say something derogatory about his upbringing but I know his folks were decent people who just didn't have any training in dealing with anomalies of Nature except to "knock 'em in the head." Repeated applications of this maxim had not had a salutary effect on Earl's personality and had actually made him quite resistant to physical duress. I remember when our pastor, Brother Davis, had a tent preacher come through town who stayed on for a couple of days to attend a big baptism down on the Blackwater. Earl was about eleven then and needed the Spirit worse than just about anyone around so he was hauled down to the river to get dunked.

However, he was not in the good graces of Brother Davis for a number of reasons, the most recent being a stunt that he had pulled only a couple of months prior. Instead of being in church, Earl had snuck off and gone over to Brother Davis' place just west of town. Rev. Davis had a good boar named Jake that he used to put out at stud and it made him a fair bit of money when that was pretty hard to come by. Earl had been saying that the preacher's boar was big enough to throw a saddle on and ride to a standstill, and on that hot, still, dry Sunday morning he aimed to prove it. Earl got a rope around the boar's neck and snubbed it to a post where he threw little

71

Virgie Davis' pony saddle on the monster. A quick yank on the rope and he was off, galloping across the hog lot raising seven kinds of hell.

Unfortunately it was hot and it was dry and hogs don't sweat, contrary to the popular saying, so it lay down and died. Earl hadn't counted on that and now he had a five hundred pound ham saddled up and going nowhere. He thought the best solution would be to get rid of the evidence by making it look like an accident, which would have worked if he had only put the saddle back and walked away. But Earl liked to do things in a grand way, so he hitched up Old Jess, which had been Rev. Davis' father's old mule, retired since the old man's death, and dragged Jake back into the barn. He then went and got a gallon of fuel oil and poured it over the carcass, lit it up, and ran.

In the end, the list of casualties ran to: one boar; twelve brood sows; seven times that many pigs; 400 bales of hay; and a retired mule. Among Earl's many mistakes that morning, the biggest, aside from going there in the first place, was forgetting to remove the saddle. He was tried, convicted and sentenced to three months on a county farm hoeing weeds and moving rocks. One day he was required to clear the weeds out of a stock pond so he dumped fifty pounds of herbicide in the water killing all the fish, thirty-two head of cattle and the warden's horse. He spent a good deal of time in solitary. Earl said it was awful; reminded him of a chicken coop.

Well, that morning in the river the tent preacher had been doing most of the baptizing until it was Earl's turn. That was when Brother Davis stepped in and took over, saying that he had been waiting for this day for a while now.

He moved out into the water and beckoned Earl to come hither. Earl waded on out there and the preacher simply said, "Lord, give me strength," and with that he grabbed Earl by the neck and shoved him straight into the water and held him under. Well, Earl thrashed about for the longest time and the crowd went silent. After about two minutes, the tent preacher, realizing that Earl's conversion was about to be something other than religious, ran out there to put a stop to it.

That's when the mob turned ugly, throwing bottles and rocks and chicken bones from their picnic baskets, shouting things like,

"Leave the man alone!" and "He's doing the Lord's work!" They succeeded in stopping the tent preacher who just stood there dumbstruck with a deep cut on his scalp and half an egg salad sandwich stuck to the back of his neck.

When Brother Davis turned loose of Earl and slowly turned around, he had a heavenly smile on his face as he waded back toward the shore singing "What a Friend We Have in Jesus." Murmurs of praise began emanating from the crowd, ranging from "Hallelujah" to "Hot Damn."

Then, of a sudden, the noise faded and all eyes were on the river. Brother Davis was still singing and had his back to the river so he didn't stop until a piercing rebel yell split the air. "Holy shit! I've seen the light!" Earl had risen up out of the water like the Phoenix itself and was rushing toward the shore waving his arms and slobbering on himself. Old brother Davis turned around to look and just collapsed right there in the water. They hauled him out and he came to momentarily, uttered his last words, and died.

Unfortunately, Earl admitted to us later that he had played dead so the preacher would let go of him, so we knew him for what he was. The old folks, though, thought there was something strange and unexplainable about him, which he used to his advantage when he ran for sheriff. He would stand out on somebody's farm, chew on a toothpick, look sideways at them, and say something like, "You sure got a lot of nice stuff here. I'd hate to see anything happen to it. Hope I get elected."

So, when I got fired it was kind of a blessing because it meant that I didn't have to work under Earl Cutberth, but it did mean that I had to look for something else. I could have worked as a farm laborer for four bits a day, hauled hay for a half cent a bale, or gotten a ten pound sack of flour for voting Democratic. Johnson County Missouri in 1933 was what they now call "economically disadvantaged" and had been so for a very long time.

I started thinking about some way to put my years in law-enforcement to work and keep doing what I'd always done, only privately. I opened up a little storefront on West Pine St. just up from the grain elevator and began advertising myself as a private eye.

The first few cases were pretty simple. I found Noah Sneed's prize bull on his own property. I got three chickens and a bushel basket of tomatoes for that. I found the widow Green's cat drying in the sun on a gravel road. I didn't get anything for that. And I found old Mrs. Falkenberry who had wandered off again, two miles south of town asking a mailbox for directions to Knob Knoster. I got supper from her daughter for that. I also got treated to the sight of the old lady in the nude when she walked out of her bedroom calling for someone named Roy. Her deceased husband had been named Bill.

Then one day I got a telephone call from a woman who had read my modest advertisement in the paper and wanted to come in for a consultation. She said her name was Miss Delion and that the matter was somewhat urgent. I liked the sound of her and wondered what she might look like. She had an elegant voice and a level of sophistication that one didn't find very often in our part of the world. Her name even sounded exotic. She was to come over that evening at five and so I had all day to get ready for her. I swept and dusted and got everything looking just right and at a about a quarter to five came a knock on the door. I straightened my necktie and took a last glance in the mirror, then headed for the door. "Miss Delion, please come in," I said as I opened the door with as much composure as I could. The sight before me, however, was not what I had expected. In fact it wasn't Miss Delion. It was my brother.

"Miss who?" he asked.

"Miss nobody. She's a client and I'm expecting her at any moment."

"Well I ought to stick around and meet her, don't you think?"

"Get out," I said.

He missed the subtlety and walked in anyway, sat down behind my desk and helped himself to a cigarette. "Damn, you got coffee made. Why don't you pour me a cup?" he asked.

"It's not for you, it's for my client" I replied.

He arose ceremoniously and walked over to the cabinet, took down a cup and had just begun to pour it himself when a voice said, "Mr. Cutberth?"

"Yes," we answered in unison and turned to face the door.

"I'm Sheriff Cutberth," he said, looking her up and down.

"I'm Vern Cutberth. Miss, is there something I can do for you?" I asked.

74

"I'm Miss Delion," she said.

"I'm sorry, I was expecting someone older," I said, blinking hard to clear my eyes. "Please sit down." She couldn't have been more than seventeen or eighteen.

"I'm older than I look," she said confidently.

"Sheriff," I said with a dismissive waive, "if you don't mind, this meeting is strictly confidential." He was blowing smoke rings and staring at her rear end. He had made no effort to move. "Confidential means that you can't listen to what we're talking about," I said slowly and patiently.

"Oh, so I gotta git," he said at last.

"That's right Earl, you gotta git." He filched another cigarette, strode toward the door with a backward glance at Miss Delion's buttocks, and walked up the street with one of my good cups. I watched him walk around the corner, through the open window over my shoulder, before turning back to my "client."

She spoke, "He's not right, is he?"

"I'm afraid not," I answered, avoiding her eyes. "Now what can I do for you?"

She took a picture out of a bag and laid it on my desk. It showed a young man holding up two other photographs, one in each hand. I couldn't make them out.

"This man took something from me and I want him back. Look at it as a sort of manhunt if you wish."

"What's his name and what did he take?"

"His name is Thomas Elliot and what he took is not important. I'm really only interested in his return," she said.

I could only imagine one thing that a man would take from a girl her age and there was no getting it back. "Well . . . yes, we'll leave that unsaid," I stammered. "Now, do you have any idea where he might be?"

"I have a pretty good idea. His people come from Douglas County near a village called Goodville."

"I've never heard of it," I said.

"That's not surprising. It is quite remote," she replied.

I couldn't get past her demeanor. She acted so much older than she looked. She had straight, black hair and high cheekbones, a lovely olive complexion and deep, dark eyes. I wondered if she might have had Indian blood in her background. Her sophistication coupled with her good looks was beginning to make me nervous and causing me to wish that my chuckleheaded brother had stayed.

"So, do your parents know about this man?" I gently queried.

"My parents are dead," she said without feeling.

"I'm sorry to hear that."

"I lost them many years ago," she said dryly.

"Well," I said, probing further, "you don't seem like you're from around here."

"I was born in the West Indies, actually."

"Is that where your parents were from?"

"My mother was but my father was from Spain, originally."

"So, when did you come to the United States?" I asked, wanting to take notes.

"My mother and I emigrated to Florida after my father died."

"So what brings you to this part of the world?"

"Mister Elliot. I knew he was from Douglas County, Missouri and I have come here in hopes of finding him."

"Why didn't you just go to Douglas County to find him?" I felt foolish because I already knew the answer. It had one paved road leading in. If you could find your way back to it, it would lead you out.

"As I said, it is remote. Besides, I doubt if I could persuade the local authorities to assist me in my efforts."

Of this I was sure. Douglas County was no place for a lady in 1933. It still isn't in 2003. I got as much information from her as I could. She didn't want to talk much about her past or her family. She didn't even want to talk too much about the elusive Mr. Elliot, but I began to understand her maturity, losing her mother and father, emigrating to a new a country, being taken advantage of by this deadbeat hillbilly. I was pleased on my part and relieved on hers to find out that she had been left with ample means of support.

After bidding her farewell and closing the door, I poured a cup of coffee and sat back at my desk to go over the information and look at the picture again. I had just lit up a Camel and reared back in my chair when a voice from Hell rang out in my ear. "The bastard got to her didn't he?!" I whirled around to see Earl's face framed in my windowpane, grinning like a fool. He was wearing the same glazed expression that he was wearing when we'd catch him playing with himself in the barn loft. I hit him in the face. He went down and was silent for a long time.

I finished my coffee and pondered my strategy. I could write the officials at the Douglas County courthouse, or perhaps contact someone in Goodville myself. Alternatively, I could go there. I was sure that they wouldn't have helped her and I wasn't too sure that I wouldn't be rebuffed as well. Hillbillies just didn't like outsiders, and though they killed each other on a regular basis, they hated "foreigners" more and would likely be less than helpful. I wasn't going to get anywhere by correspondence. I would have to make the journey.

I was immersed in thought and had begun to examine the picture again when I heard a rustling in the grass outside my window. I heard muffled curses and then my brother's voice. "Somebody's going to have to go with you! You can't go down there by yourself!" It was hard to understand him but when he hauled himself back up in the window I understood why. He was missing a tooth and his top lip was split all the way to his left nostril so when he spoke the air whistled through the gap, causing the cleft in his lip to flap open and shut.

I thought he looked better. "You're not going with me," I said, "And you'd better get Doc to sew up that lip up before the pain sets in."

"I am too going with you! . . . and the pain's done set in," he flapped and whistled. "How long I been out?" he asked.

"I don't know, five, ten minutes."

I made some notes, then carefully placed all the information in a manila envelope and walked out.

He followed me up the road and onto Holden Street still talking about how he should be allowed to go. "But who would be sheriff while you're gone?" I asked.

"Gene?" he said hopefully. Gene Daly had been in jail so often he had become a trustee.

"You left him in charge before when you went up to West Quincy for a week on that 'fishing trip.'" West Quincy, Missouri was then the whorehouse capital of the state. The whole main street was lined with them.

"I don't remember that good but it seemed to me he did all right," Earl replied timidly.

"You don't remember because you were gone, you were drunk, and you were shacked up at Big Fay's having the time of your life."

"Well, yeah" he said, crossing his eyes just like he used to when we'd catch him stuffing acorns up his nose.

He was about to say something when I opened a door and pushed him inside.

"Howdy Mavis," I said to the nurse.

"Hey Mavis," whistled Earl.

"Hi boys. Doc will be with you in a minute or two." I tipped my hat and walked out. I heard Nurse Childs ask Earl who had done the damage this time. "Him," he said as the door closed.

I walked straight to my office, into the back room that served as my living quarters. I knew it would take awhile for old Doc to get Earl stitched back into place, but I packed and hastily left town without being noticed, just in case. To avoid being chased down by Earl, I stayed off Highway 13, chose dirt roads that were protected on at least one side by trees, got out and switched the ground with a branch to obscure my tracks whenever I made a turn, and seriously thought about dynamiting the bridge across the Osage River.

The trip through the Ozarks is a story in itself but in the end I did reach Douglas County. I emerged from a hollow with no car, no bags, no money, no gun, tattered clothes, stick-tights and cuckle-burrs all over me, a couple of hickeys left by leeches and a snakebite wound that I hoped wouldn't be fatal.

I strode into Goodville somewhat knowing that, while I would be noticed as a stranger, I had acquired the appearance of a real hillbilly, a fact that I had hoped would open a few doors. Unfortunately, Goodville only had six doors, although there were half again as many doorways. I made for a building that had a chance of being something because it was made of stone. The sign on the façade was faded and read, "Goodville, Missouri Est . . ." I couldn't make out the year because it was either faded or had been rubbed out. In any event I didn't care. I pushed open the door and entered.

It was dark inside and smelled unused. I tried to find a lamp but kept bumping into things. I didn't have any matches and was hoping to find some. Then a hammer cocked off to my left.

"Who are ye and what are ye doing in here?" said a nasal voice in the darkness. "Speak up or I'll kill you dead."

I wanted to duck and slip outside but I realized that I was framed by the light from the open door behind me and didn't have a Chinaman's chance of being missed, so I spoke.

"The name's Vern Cutberth," I said slowly and with composure. I didn't want this man to think I was frightened, but nor did I want him to think I was belligerent.

"Never heard of ye," said the voice.

"I'm from up in Johnson County," I said.

"Never heard of it," said the voice.

I thought about saying that I'd never heard of his piss ant town either. But instead I just said, "I'll be damned."

"What's yer bidness here boy?" he asked.

"Looking for a man name of Thomas Elliot. You know him?"

"Maybe. Why do ye want him? What's he done?"

"Don't know. I was asked by a young lady to come and take him back to Johnson County."

"He musta got to her," the voice cackled horribly. "Tell me all 'bout it and I might tell ye what I know about him."

This fellow would have gotten along well with my brother, I thought.

"Don't know any details. She wouldn't say," I replied.

"Well that's because ye don't know nothing about them there interrogation techniques like you would a if you was a high-powered lawman like me. Hell, I found a buried treasure once. Done it by my own wits," came the mysterious voice. "You ever done somethin' like that?"

"I'm going to kick your ass," I blurted, and crossed the room quickly, in the direction of the voice. I swung my fist as hard as I could and connected with a skull that must have belonged to a buffalo, it was so hard. The voice went silent as the man hit the ground. I rummaged through his pockets and found some matches, then went round the room looking for a lamp. I found one and lit it up. Going back to the prostrate man, I searched him for other things I needed and found a pack of cigarettes. I lit one and walked over to the desk that sat in the middle of the room. Apparently, I was in what passed for city hall.

I had lost everything on the way down and had no idea where to begin looking for my man. He could be anywhere in this kingdom of trees and brush and snakes. He could be dead. He might not even be in Douglas County. I needed clues in a hurry and was hoping to find some in this building. Most of what I found was too old and too moldy to be of any use. Old newspaper clippings, deeds that I would have thought should have been filed at the county courthouse, an empty perfume bottle of all things, and . . . a key! "Keys are good," I thought to myself, "but what does this one open?" I looked around for a filing cabinet, a safe, anything. There was nothing to be found that even had a lock on it.

I decided to search the other buildings for signs of life and locks, so I pocketed the key, picked up the lantern in one hand, then searched around for the pistol. I retrieved it and went out the door into the street. The first building east of city hall was a wooden structure with no door. I stepped inside. The walls were covered with shelves and behind a counter was a box of cubicles that had probably been used by the mail service. It looked to be an old dry goods store. I rummaged around but found nothing. There was a pile of rags in the corner like someone had been sleeping there temporarily but nothing else, not even a can of beans.

Across from the dry goods store was a ramshackle house that indeed had a door on it. I crossed the dirt-road main street and carefully, because I didn't want to fall through, eased up the steps and up to the front door. I pulled the key out of my pocket and tried the lock. The key didn't fit but the door fell backwards into the house, scaring the hell out of me.

I almost discharged the gun into my foot like Earl had done the week after his election to sheriff. Holding the lantern up, I went in. I stood in the middle of a front room with two other rooms off it. The inside of the house smelled like rotting meat; I had to hold my breath. I was becoming afraid and wished I had stayed in Johnson County and told the Delion girl to go elsewhere.

There was a table against one wall that had three plates on it. Two were covered in dust and there was food running down the sides of the table legs. The third plate was equally dusty around the edges but had a clean place right in the middle of it. Someone had been eating off the plate and flies were gathered in its center. I heard a creek in the floorboards and a loud snap followed by a scream. I cocked the gun and whirled around to see the city hall man standing knee deep in broken floorboards on the porch.

"Don't shoot!" he yelled.

After my heart came down out of my throat, I walked over and stood in the doorway just staring at him like a man stares at the bottom of his shoe after he steps in dog shit.

"How long was I out?" he asked.

"I don't know," I said, "my watch is broken," then added impatiently, "Well, get out of the hole, jackass."

"I can't," he winced, "I think my ankle's broke."

"Your head's going to be broke if you ever scare me like that again," I said, without humor.

"I got here yesterday and there weren't nobody in town so I thought I'd just wait on you. I figured you'd get here sooner or later. What the hell happened to you?" he sat down and pulled his foot out of the hole.

"It's a long story. You don't want to know," I said, not caring to fill him in on the details so that he could ridicule *me* for a change. "How did you get in here?" I looked around for some means of transportation.

"I left the car up on 60 and bought a mule off this old man. It's thirteen miles on that road there that ain't no bigger than a cow path. Took me best part of a day."

"Where is it?" I asked.

"Hell, man, you're looking at it. You crossed it to get in here," he said incredulously.

"The mule," I said.

"Oh, I don't know. I think it wandered off last night. I was sleeping in that old store across the road and when I woke up it was gone."

"Stolen, probably." I knelt down to examine Earl's leg. It wasn't broken but he was going to have trouble walking on it.

"Who could have stole it? Hell, there ain't nobody lives in this town, I don't reckon," he said.

"If you can stand up, follow me," I said.

I helped Earl to his feet and into the house. The smell of rotting flesh hit us both in the face. "What died in here?" asked Earl.

"I don't know, but we ought to find out. Might be our man," I said, hoping so. I really wanted to get the hell out of Goodville and if it meant finding Thomas Elliot dead then that would be fine. Someone or something was going back to dust in this house and it might just as well have been Elliot as somebody else.

We looked all round the house and still couldn't find the source of the stench. We figured it must be under the floor. I was about to go outside and take a look when Earl pointed toward a thin rope made from knotted rags hanging from the ceiling. We gave it a yank and a swarm of flies rushed down on us. The freshly intensified smell was almost too much to bear. I took the lantern away from Earl and started up the ladder. After a quick look around I slid down the stairs, grabbed Earl and told him that we had to get the hell out of there. For once he didn't argue and we made for the door. I have never been so frightened. The flesh on my neck was crawling as we hobbled out into the street and away from the house.

"What'd ya see up there, Vern?" he asked, now about as frightened as me.

"I found your mule," I said out of breath, "and there's more."

"More mules?" he asked, open-mouthed.

"People," I panted, "dead ones, all lined up and hanging from the rafters. The mule's at the front and somebody's been eating off it, but then there are the people. The fresher ones are toward the front and the ones in the back are skin and bones. Somebody's been eating off of them too!"

"There's boogers down here, Vern," my brother said, grasping my shoulder. I was too frightened to tell him to remove his hand.

"Boogers don't exist, Earl. They're a figment of the imagination. But there is one hell of a bad man out here somewhere," I said with confidence.

"Naw sir," said Earl, "there's a booger fer sure. The Booger of Rotten Bottom, they call it."

"The Booger of Rotten Bottom?" I asked, trembling. "Where did you hear a story like that?"

"From that old man I bought the mule from. He said there was a booger lived down in the Rotten Bottom of Clifty Creek and that all the people who was here is gone and all that comes in here don't never come back." I could feel him shudder through his hand on my shoulder.

"Damn!" I cursed. "Why'd you come down in here after hearing that?"

"Well hell, bubba, somebody's got to look after you. I couldn't let you walk into something like that all by yourself," he said earnestly.

I looked at him for a minute and saw something akin to human decency on his face, the kind of look like he had the time he let Grandma Cutberth get out of the privy and back in the house before pulling it over.

"Thanks Earl," I said, touched.

"And I figured, there must be some treasure involved and I sure as hell wasn't gonna let you git all of it fer yourself," he cackled, bobbing his head up and down.

"Right," I said, now back in control of my emotions. "We've got four hours of daylight left and I want to put as much distance between us and this place as we can before nightfall."

"I'm with you, but how we going to do it? You ain't going to be able to carry me and the chest both. That sonofabitch is hea..." he stopped mid-word.

"What chest?" I asked, staring him in the eyes.

He looked around sort of panicky.

"Earl! You're about to piss me off. I'll ask you again. What chest!?"

"Well," he began, with that hangdog look he got whenever he'd been caught. "I found this here chest over there in the city hall and I shot at the lock and then I shot at the hinges and the bullet ricocheted off and damned near got me, so I thought I'd best stop. So, I buried it out back of the city hall and put this big old rock on it." He shrugged as though it was something he did everyday. Actually, in his case, it probably was.

"When were you planning on telling me about the chest, Earl. Ever?"

"Well, I knew you was gonna be too busy looking for this Elliot fella to care a damn about some old chest, so I thought I'd come back down another time and pick it up."

* * *

83

Earl kept looking at me and saying, "What?" but I just kept saying, "Dig."

We got the small chest up out of the ground and I pulled the key out of my pocket, held it up and blew the dust off it. Earl's mouth dropped open as the key slid neatly into the lock and the chest opened without a creak. "When was you going to tell me about this damned key?"

"Shut up Earl," I said impatiently. What I saw was like nothing I'd ever seen before and nothing I've ever seen since. I was nearly blinded by the brilliance: gold jewelry, diamonds, old coins. Earl was breathing so hard I thought he was going to hyperventilate.

I couldn't believe my eyes. Earl couldn't keep his slobber in his mouth. We were so engrossed by this find that we had entirely forgotten the Booger of Rotten Bottom and the danger that approaching nightfall would bring. I began emptying the contents of the chest and mentally cataloguing them for the future. I knew there was no way we were going to be able to carry all of this out of here, though I knew Earl was going to fight me over it.

At the bottom of the chest, among the last few items, I found a perfume bottle exactly like the one in the desk drawer of the city hall. This one had a tiny little bit left in it. On the very bottom, like a liner, were two photographs. One was identical to the one Miss Delion had shown me which I lost on the way down. The other was a closeup of what he was holding, two photographs. They were both pictures of what looked like Miss Delion in two different dresses.

I took the photos and put them back in the chest along with the perfume bottle and then started to sort through the treasure. I tried to explain to Earl that we could only carry a few items and still make it out of here before sundown. He argued like I knew he would.

Ten minutes later he said, "So, how long was I out?"

"Not long," I said as I closed the lid on the chest and helped him to his feet, "But we've got to get moving." While Earl was unconscious I had taken his pistol and gone back through the other buildings to see what I could find. I came up with a bit of rope which Earl used to secure the little chest to my back. I had also found a corn knife that came in handy to fashion a makeshift crutch for Earl. Then I thrust the corn knife into my belt and we set off up the road.

The path went north and for the most part followed the ridges, which was good for us. I couldn't get far enough away fast enough to feel relieved but Earl was in good spirits in spite of his pain. And then night fell.

Night in the Ozark hills is night, even on a ridge, and we thought we heard the Booger in every owl's screech and coyote's howl. The wind completely died and all was still except for the sounds of wild animals and our own footsteps on the rocky path.

"Wouldn't it be hell," Earl said in a whisper.

"What would?" I replied, afraid to ask.

"You know, if we got et by a wild boar or some big ol' wampus kitty or somethin' before we got a chance to sell this treasure."

"It would really be hell if the Booger heard us talking and ate us before I got a chance to choke your chicken neck like I'm going to do if you don't shut up."

That scared him enough to make him pipe down, though he kept looking over at me like he wanted to say something. I ignored him and we kept walking.

A couple of times that night we heard sounds that sounded human, but not really human, if you know what I mean. Imagine a bear's growl mixed with the scream of a hysterical woman. The first time we heard it we nearly died of fright. The second time was just about as bad as the first, but it was farther off so we consoled ourselves with the thought that it might be going the other way and would not cross our path at all.

We walked all night long, and at some point had crossed over into Wright County because we broke through some brush to find ourselves on the edge of a town called Mountain Grove.

"We're here!" shouted Earl. "This is where I got the mule from," he said as he started picking up speed.

I picked up my pace as well, not fully believing our good fortune.

"I parked over here," he said as we rounded the corner of the Wright County Courthouse Square. A large group of people was standing around in the grass in front of the courthouse, and I heard women crying and a church bell begin to ring. We made our way toward the men and Earl's car and then saw what they had been looking at.

There was a form on the ground. It had two arms and two legs but its head had been severed. The head looked vaguely human but with pointed ears, snow-white hair and the face of a rat or a monkey. I couldn't tell because it had been shot up pretty badly. I moved in for a closer look.

"It's the Booger of Rotten Bottom," said the old man who had sold Earl the mule. "He come in town 'bout two hour ago and was a goin' from house to house like he 'uz a lookin' fer sumthin'. He done killt ten fer he got it hisself."

I had a feeling I knew what he'd been looking for. I pulled my corn knife out of my belt and asked if any man would mind if I took his left hand back to Kansas City for examination. Nobody minded and so I hacked it off his wrist and wrapped it in Earl's handkerchief.

I went to Kansas City after we got home and I had gotten a shave and some clean clothes. Two days later I contacted Miss Delion at the hotel where she was staying. She came to my office. Earl wanted to be there when she came in and after all we'd been through I supposed that it wasn't going to hurt anything.

She arrived shortly after dinner, about one o'clock. I welcomed her in and Earl poured us all a cup of coffee. "So, where is Mr. Elliot?" she asked.

"I'm afraid he's dead," I said flatly.

"Do you have any proof of this?"

"Earl," I said. He produced a jar of formaldehyde, which contained the hand of the Booger. It was covered with fine white hairs and traces of blood could still be seen under its fingernails. It had a large pink scar in the shape of a half moon on the back. "Mr. Elliot's hand."

"I see." She gnawed her bottom lip. "Well then, you didn't happen to recover any of my personal effects did you?"

"I did," I answered tersely. Earl brought up the treasure chest and I opened it with my key. "I believe you will find many things missing, but we were unable to bring it all and I have no way of knowing how much was originally there. I hope you will trust me on this."

"I do. I do. But there seems to be one thing of a very personal

86

nature still missing."

"It wouldn't be this?" I pulled the perfume bottle out of the top drawer of my desk.

"Oh yes," she answered excitedly, taking it in her hand. "There was another one as well. Where is it?"

"I'm afraid it was empty so we left it."

"Are you *sure* it was empty?"

"Quite sure."

"Very well then, I suppose our business is done. I shall pay you now for your services and be on my way."

She made out a check and I watched her sign her name. She had faltered for a second, then signed *Juanita Delion*.

"Thank you, Miss Delion, for your business," I said cordially, then stopped as she began to rise.

"I'm afraid there's one more thing to be discussed," I said, and drew the photos from my drawer. She recognized the first as the one she had given me. Then she recoiled a bit when she saw the second, enlarged picture of the photos in Elliot's hand.

"Would you care to comment on these?" I asked quietly.

"They're merely picture portraits of me. That's why I didn't mention them before. Remember that you were looking for Mr. Elliot. You *knew* where *I* was."

"Could you tell me why in one portrait you are dressed in the manner of a Victorian housewife and in the second in a dress popular at the turn of the century, both many years before your time?"

She turned and looked at Earl who had been staring at her backside. "He's a very disturbed man," she said with disgust.

"I would have to agree, but he isn't the only one here who isn't right."

"I don't know what you mean," she said, getting defensive, "I hired you to do a task which you have completed to my satisfaction and I see no reason why I should be under any obligation to explain myself. I simply like to dress in outmoded fashions. And while that may seem frivolous or eccentric to you, it is none of your business. Now, good day." She rose abruptly and turned but Earl blocked her way.

"Not so fast," I said. "Would you mind explaining why, in these photos, enlarged again, the date on the left photograph reads 'July 15, 1869'?"

She looked intently at the picture.

"Would you also like to know how I knew that this disgusting figure of a hand belonged to Mr. Elliot?" She said nothing. "Because in the second photo, which I retrieved from your chest, a half-moon scar is clearly visible, whereas in the first photo, the hand is too small to see. You never mentioned this identifying mark to me." I calmed down slightly and carried on. She stood there speechless and stared at me with hate.

"Upon my return, I went to Kansas City, on a hunch. I had the artifacts identified as Spanish, fifteenth century. The perfume was unidentifiable. I had the photos enlarged. And I took a little trip to the library. It all adds up to the same thing. And now I want you to tell me who you really are, Miss Delion, or should I say, Miss de Leon, as in Ponce de Leon. Juan Ponce de Leon perished in Cuba from his wounds following a battle with Florida Indians in 1521. He was looking for the Fountain of Youth. He thought it was on the island of Bimini, just north of Hispaniola. Is it?"

"The whereabouts of the Fons Juventutis are unknown even by me," she said at last, "but in five hundred years I have never ceased to be amazed at the stupidity of men. You don't stop until you've ruined everything, including yourselves. You dig and dig and dig and then one day you uncover a demon that devours you because you have only the capacity to pry, not the capacity to understand or the ability to manage."

"Tell me about Elliot," I said, no more interested in being nagged by a five hundred year old woman than any other.

"He found my secret, he tried to blackmail me, then fled with half of the potion of youth because he was more interested in eternal life than money, which I would have gladly kept paying, by the way. He was a fool," she laughed.

"There were two bottles," I said, "it looks to me like he got it all."

"Not half the quantity," she replied. "Half the potion. You see, he only had the part that immortalizes the body. The other half binds the soul to it. Without the second half," she said slowly producing another bottle from the under the neckline of her dress. "The soul eventually passes into the hands of God, even though the body remains alive. You see," she went on, "a man without a soul is an empty vessel and there are many dark and hungry spirits who would wish to take up residence in it."

"What now?" I asked, suddenly afraid of my knowledge. Perhaps she was right about men after all.

"That is up to you," she said, pulling a revolver from her purse. "Entirely up to you."

Well, I am not going to go into the details of the negotiations that followed. The fact is that we all got something in the end and, hell, I'm still around to tell the story aren't I? She walked out of the office that day and neither Earl nor I have ever seen her since. We just sat there staring out the window, wondering about how strange life was, and had been, and was going to be.

Earl lit up a smoke and reared back in his chair. "I'll bet she could teach a feller a thing or two," he cackled in that tone of voice he used just before he'd get slapped. "Hell of an ass on her," he said, "you know, for an old broad."

"Shut up, Earl," I said.

"I'm telling you, someday we'll all wake up murdered in our beds."

OHMIGOD, NOT ANOTHER ONE
Jeanie Stewart

Head librarian, Lenore Hacker, winced as Carly Burnbow crashed the metal book truck into the side of the polished mahogany circulation desk.

"Ohmigod!" Carly shrieked. Her voice, echoing through the quiet library, was every bit as annoying as her treatment of the antique furniture.

Lenore pushed her reading glasses to the top of her head and scowled at her rotund helper.

Carly giggled. "I guess I need better brakes on this thing." She reversed the cart an inch, shrugged, then held up a worn copy of *Death Lurks*. "I shelved all the books except this one. Where did you say it goes again?"

"Fiction section, dear," Lenore said with a tired sigh. "Alphabetically by the author's last name."

"But which author? It has two— "

"But both of them have the same *last* name, don't they?" Lenore tapped her finger against the spine of the book. "Just go by whatever letter is typed on the label here."

Carly slapped a pudgy palm against her forehead.

"Ohmigod! I should have known that!"

Carly's expletive-of-choice always sent a shiver up Lenore's spine. But it seemed to be the way young people talked nowadays. Disrespect was the rule, be it for deity, age, or even the English language.

"Don't look so disgusted, Miss Hacker. Remember, I've only been here a few months. I'll catch on . . . eventually."

Lenore doubted it. Carly Burnbow was not exactly the crispest book on the shelf. She had been helping out at the Pottsville Public Library three nights a week since her graduation from high school four months ago, and in all that time the only thing she'd mastered was the art of annoying her boss. Lenore would have fired her that very first week if the library board hadn't vetoed the idea. The fresh young board president claimed that he didn't want Lenore uptown all alone on the nights the library stayed open late. But Lenore knew the real reason he insisted she hire the ditzy child. The board felt that Lenore Hacker was getting way too old to run the library. Lenore's jaw tightened involuntarily. Well, if they planned to groom Carly as her replacement, they had a long, long way to go.

Carly patted Lenore's hand. "Don't frown, you sweet old thing. Just be patient. By the time I've been here as long as you, I'll know everything there is to know about this library stuff."

"Of course you will, dear." Lenore gave her best grandmotherly nod. There was no sense in telling the child that she would never be here that long.

"How long *have* you worked here, Miss Hacker? My mama says that you were the librarian way back when she was a little girl. She says you were even ol—" Carly broke off her chatter and at least had the decency to blush. Not many young people did anymore.

"Age is relative and children don't always perceive things exactly as they are," Lenore said.

"Huh?"

"The young see things from their own special perspective."

Carly cocked her head sideways, twined a lock of mauve hair around a finger, and stared blankly.

"Let me put it this way. To a child any grownup is old. Someone twenty is old. Someone seventy is old. Children don't really make a distinction."

"Ohmigod! That's *so* true. I used to think my mom was like . . . really, really old. And now she doesn't seem that old at all."

"Children have funny ideas sometime."

"That's for sure. You know what I used to think when my mom would bring me to the library? I know this is really silly, but I used to think that you lived here. Like you weren't a real person at all. When the lights went out, you just jumped in the file cabinet or went down to the basement or something 'til morning."

The library's massive brass door opened and a gush of smoky autumn air fluttered the magazines on the nearby rack. A thin young man of no more than twenty stepped inside and gazed around with wild eyes, as if he had just arrived on the planet. From the looks of him, maybe he had. He wore tattered baggy jeans and a filthy black T-shirt that proposed an act Lenore could only hope had something to do with today's music scene.

92

"Ohmigod," Carly said, rolling her eyes. "Not another one!"

The boy smoothed down his windblown hair, which was black at the roots, but variegated down to a fried, frizzly, unnatural yellow at his shoulders. His pale skin was plastered with tattoos.

Carly wrinkled up her nose and leaned close to Lenore's ear. "Pothead," she whispered. "I can smell it all the way over here."

"Can we help you?" Lenore asked, ignoring Carly as much as possible. Her eyes were drawn to the row of skull earrings that dangled from the young man's ear.

"Yeah," he growled. "I want a li-bary card."

Lenore handed him the required form, which he carried over to the nearest table and began laboriously filling out.

"I can't stand those people," Carly whispered. "Ever since that detox center opened, the whole town has been overrun by scum like that! I don't think they should be allowed to come in here."

"Carly, this is a *public* library. That means it's here for everyone."

"But it shouldn't be for them! They've ruined our town. Don't you ever read the police reports in the paper? No one is safe around here anymore. I'm telling you, someday we'll all wake up murdered in our beds."

Pointing out the absurdity of her words would have been a waste of breath, so Lenore bit her cheek and let Carly prattle on.

"The cops gather up crooks and druggies from all over the state and then instead of locking them up the way they should, they ship them down here to us and then those detox people just let them run free all over town!" She crossed her arms over her chest and scowled as the young man reappeared with his finished form.

Lenore took the form and strained to read the scratchy writing. "OK . . . Wayne. Is there anything in particular we can help you find tonight?"

He shrugged. "Nope, just looking for some books."

"Duh!" Carly sneered.

Lenore sent an icy look in her direction.

"Sorry," Carly muttered.

"Are you looking for any particular books?" Lenore asked Wayne.

"Nope. I'll just look around." His gaze darted around the library's dim interior. "Where's your real stuff? You know, true, not made-up."

"The non-fiction stacks are on the left side of that reading table."

He'd hardly had time to amble out of earshot when Carly started up again. "I'll bet you ten bucks he wants a book on Hitler or the occult. It's all his type ever read."

"Stereotyping people is a very bad habit, Carly."

"Don't feed me that old line about you can't judge a book by its cover. You just watch. You'll see I'm right. Either that, or he'll get a chemistry book."

"Chemistry?"

"Yeah, you know. So he can look up how to make a bomb or open a meth lab or something."

"You mustn't be so judgmental. You don't know he's from the detox. And even if he is, everyone deserves a chance to break free of their demon . . . whatever form they take."

"Everybody deserves a chance to feel safe in their own home too, but I don't. Not since *those* people came," Carly said. "And I can't believe you're taking this so lightly. Didn't you hear about old Mrs. Reedman? Just last week she was attacked . . . right in her own bedroom. Anyone with half a brain would know an old lady like that wouldn't have money, but they were just looking for anything they could steal and sell for money to buy drugs."

"Did Treece catch who did it?"

Carly shook her head. "My mama says our chief of police couldn't catch a cold in a lizard."

"I think you mean 'in a blizzard', dear."

Carly rolled her eyes. "Whatever," she said. "But no, he didn't catch anybody. For all you know, that could be the very guy right over there." She crooked her short little neck in the young man's direction. "It's disgusting. And Ms. Reedman . . . not only was she robbed, but she was . . . well, she was nearly killed. She's still in intensive care, you know." Carly picked up *Death Lurks* and waved it angrily. "I guess I'll go shelve this. You can wait on the druggie creep."

Suddenly the door swooshed open again. Carly jumped a foot off the floor—which was an amazing feat considering her weight and the fact that twelve inches was almost a quarter of her total height.

94

"Ohmigod, Harlan," she squealed. "You nearly scared the pee outta me!"

Harlan, Carly's husband of two months, held the door open and motioned impatiently. "C'mon, Car. It's nine o'clock and I'm starving. I already called ahead to Pizza Hut . . . our pie will be ready in about five minutes."

Carly looked back at Lenore, then at the young man wandering aimlessly among the shelves. "Uh . . . I don't know, Har. I uh . . ."

"You go on," Lanore said, dismissing her with a wave. "I don't imagine pizza is very good once it gets cold."

Carly put a hand to the side of her mouth as if that would muffle her voice. "But are you *sure* you'll be all right? I mean . . . I don't want to leave you here all alone with that weirdo."

"I'll be fine," Lenore said. "I've been closing up this library for more years that you've been alive."

"But . . ."

"Don't argue, young lady. He's just a boy wanting books. You know what I always say, anyone who loves books can't be all bad."

Lenore could almost see Carly's brain processing the information. If Carly had been a cartoon, a little scale would have appeared over her head with a slice of cold pizza on one side and a blood-drenched old lady on the other.

Harlan tipped the scale. "C'mon, girl. I left the truck running."

Lenore picked up the day's circulation tally sheet. "Go on, don't worry about me. I won't be much longer."

Carly dropped *Death Lurks* onto a nearby table and followed Harlan. But no sooner had the door clanged shut, than a shadow fell across the circulation desk.

"Ah-hem." Wayne cleared his throat. "Now that the snooty chick is gone, maybe you can help me." He scratched an armpit. "You got any books on magic?"

Lenore brushed nonexistent wrinkles from her tweed skirt and came around the edge of the desk. "You mean stage magic? Illusions? Magicians, that sort of thing?"

"Yeah, I guess."

"Follow me." As Lenore walked toward the stacks, her crepe-soled shoes made no sound on the dark green industrial-strength carpet, but she could hear Wayne's shuffling step behind her.

When he suddenly laid his bony hand on her shoulders, she spun around so quickly they both nearly toppled over.

"I don't really want books about magicians," he said.

He was tall, but so was Lenore. Despite her age-stooped shoulders, they were still practically nose-to-nose. She gazed into his face. "Your eyes are very bloodshot, young man. You should take better care of yourself."

"I just love how everybody in this hick town wants to be my mama and tell me what to do," he sneered.

Lenore backed up a step. "What is it that you *really* want, Wayne?"

"I uh . . . well, I really want a book that has . . . you know, spells and stuff."

"I see. Then you're looking for books about black magic and the occult."

"Yeah, I . . . I guess so." Despite his awkward stammering, his eyes never left hers.

"I'm sorry, Wayne, but the library can't keep books like that. City policy. This is a very conservative town. You can just imagine the trouble it'd cause if some love-starved teenager took home a book, lit some candles, and whipped up a love potion. The minute her mother caught her, we'd be having a town meeting. Before you know it, I'd lose my job."

"Yeah, I guess you're right." He looked disappointed.

Lenore pinched her lips together. She could see that it was just another disappointment in a long line of disappointments that had made up this young man's life. She lowered her voice to a conspiratorial tone. "Censorship is a terrible thing, don't you agree?"

He nodded.

"I'll tell you what I can do. I have some books that might interest you in my private collection."

He brightened visibly. "Cool."

"They're in my office." She glanced at her watch. "It's closing time, but if you want, you can look through them while I finish my paperwork and lock up for the night."

She opened the door to her office and let Wayne inside. "They're in that cabinet on the far wall. Help yourself. I'll be back in a few minutes."

Only when she reached out to turn off the buzzing fluorescents in the back of the library did she realize how her hands were trembling.

Not from fear—but from excitement. She clicked off the heater and headed back toward her office. Unlike Carly, Lenore didn't mind that the drug rehabilitation center had come to town. As far as she was concerned it was a vast storehouse of unwanted, unloved people . . . her favorite kind . . . the ones nobody missed.

Hand on the doorknob, she smiled, freeing her elongated canine teeth, which had been throbbing against her cheeks from the moment the young man had walked into her lair. Silently she slipped into her office.

"Ohmigod," was all Wayne had time to say.

He had only the rudiments of
dementia, but don't we all?

TO LIVE IN THE NICK OF TIME
Donn Irving

The sergeant of police told it to me: two boys hunting squirrels had found the head. He described something gray and drawn, puckered like a fig, said it was found stuffed upright into a network of roots curled out from a cutbank. Positioned to view the world right-side-up, I thought later, as if it ever could have. The face, he went on, was tough and dry, like parchment, the eyes blank and mouth agape like that of a fish on ice. They were quite some time determining to whom the head belonged—once, when the head was part of a "whom"—and longer still finding the rest of what had belonged to the head, and the boys, though tough woodcutter's kids, had gone empty as pipped-open eggshells.

On that morning, many weeks before, I'd ridden back into town squirming in the seat, lathered in mud. Typical spring, and nothing born easily. I'd been swimming after a calf locked inside a wallowing heifer for what time seemed equivalent to the extent of her gestation up to then. Limbs had writhed about inside her, mine, the calf's, and my lower limbs slithered in a slime behind her, as though the heifer was the home and hatchery of snakes. Her exhaustion matched my own, and both of us were sculptures in clay when the dead thing arrived. Jenks, my helper in the driver's seat, and I, had a truck-cab to purge and bones to unchill.

No chance to see to the cab. The waiting room whined, groaned, growled, and coughed with pets and their people, and something else. Almost fabulous, certainly remarkable. As I peeled my mud-caked coveralls on the back porch, flat flakes of mud falling at my feet, I harkened to strumming and verses sung in a soft, soothing voice. Jenks pointed toward the sound smoothing over the others, an inscrutable smile on his face. I was so dazed that a kind of fuzzy meaninglessness permeated me, some antic indifference toward . . . practice, pressure, appointments, everything. I silently welcomed this unknown troubadour come to relate to us legends of other lands, other peoples. I wondered if my clients felt the same, then dismissed even that, them, all thought.

Sarah, my wife, came outside as usual, to brief and prepare me.

99

"Isn't he good? Matt, you've got to meet him. You will, after. This is some young man!"

"After." Always after. Clients wall to wall, like indoor kudzu.

Something folk-like, maybe a tinge of bluegrass reprising now and again. I nodded and swayed my head in tempo as I washed. I thought of a too-serious and very clinical classmate, then again on how wondrously crazy all this was. I felt magnetically drawn to my own pet-strewn music hall.

The young man I beheld held all in thrall. Faces matched their nods, their tapping feet and clapping hands. His eyes came up sidewise from his strings and fingers as I entered: Dark, bright, the eyes of a seeker of truth. His face, I remember thinking, could calm raging seas. The song he delivered sweetly, if thinly, with no hint of self-consciousness. I stood transfixed; felt transported, flown off on the wings of the music.

He finished. Sarah said: "Matt, meet Nick." My hand started forward toward the intersection, where, by tacit rules, hands meet in conventional social ways, familiar clasps, but his quickly twisted mine into a sixties grip of thumbs, then fingers and fists thrust upward. His eyes entered me. He said nothing, yet smiled perfect calm.

The music lapsed, my consciousness returned. I broke the beam from his eyes and glanced around the room. Just as I'd feared, business as usual, for I was here now to serve. The faces, with few exceptions, had grown impatient, and in some anxiety was etching like hieroglyphics. Unmistakable. Yet, no dog barked or whined, and no cat "maiiowed," and I thought once for all we know which is the savage beast. Nick's face showed me he knew me for the slave I'd become . . . and forgave me.

"Okay. Okay, we begin, but Nick, you keep singing, if you will, just until I'm caught up here." I motioned for Sarah to send the tired, the poor, the beastly-burdened and I retreated into the examination room. We're talking hinterlands here, the tiny town, the paltry and poor, and aspirated optimism.

Nick only nodded, began to chord.

I started working my way through the convocation of pets. Unlike their owners, they were by and large innocent, and, I thanked goodness or their owners' oversight in neglecting to teach them viciousness by example, tractable as well. Most was routine, the distemper and rabies variety of prevention, like an oil change or a permanent wave. Nick continued his songs. The work went efficiently.

"He's right good," said Jenks under his breath while he put a benign-looking murderous grip on the half-horse of a dog I injected . . . without a growl from either side.

I nodded, lost to the world, asleep in routine, and still half-perished from chill, but grateful for the warmth of music.

I'd carried with me into the exam room Nick's dark, lambent eyes, his disarming countenance, the grip of his hand. These blended with his songs, the lyrics resonating nostalgia and his unconsciousness of the antic ambience in which he obligingly performed. My detachment seemed complete. When Jenks flattened out the next creature, a cat, as if to stretch and skin it, I waved him off gently and twirled it about the slick table by its nape, distracting it thusly and injecting it with my free hand. It made no sound, nor stiffened. I felt it getting well, the antibiotic permeating it, for I could cure anything now, soaring toward bleary and euphoric omnipotence. Disease would, everywhere, soon be turned out to lunch.

"Where—how—did you ever learn to play like that?" I asked it of the drugs I shelved between clients, of the syringes and needles I discarded in the foot-operated can. Nick played on just beyond the door. A pair of hands clapped cadence.

I must have seen, surely, six or seven animals, all with dispatch and assuredness, their owners nameless and compliant. Reassuring to them, too, I could tell, for I felt a magnetism in each transaction, a contagious acceptance of each brief pronouncement—and their deference. Jenks eyed me, sort of askance, I saw and ignored.

"Matt," said Sarah, popping in as the last client leash-towed her stiff-legged dog toward the door, its nails susurrating over the tiles, "there's one more. Out here," and she looked kind of funny.

I'd seen the lady before. Around town. Who hadn't? Everywhere. Anywhere, it came to me now. It was like espying something in the corner of your eye while you pulled out to pass a slow-moving truck. That was the way you saw her and didn't. She walked, I recalled, holding to the grips of a cloth shopping bag she filled from here and there, from stores where she paid in coin or a crumpled bill, to cans and dumpsters where such tedium was unnecessary. She had no car, lived north of town. Somewhere. I had asked someone, once, where she walked in from. And whoever had told me: "Big house, old, just north of town, and way back from the road. And, like haunted." I'd never descried it, and who plied more roads than I? Everyone seemed to know of her, but no one I knew, knew her. None bothered.

It was the coat. Like a rainbow had bled into it. And her cloche of crimson. The blazing colors of the coat, a patchwork made as you'd make up a quilt, augmented its dominant scarlet. And that seemed reflected in her face, for she rouged her smooth cheekbones to a high tone, in the old way. Where she went, she took Mardi Gras. Youth may have once been hers, but I'd have bet it came before any roar of the twenties, yet you could not be sure exactly how you knew that. Not by her skin, certainly, for it was tight and glossy as that of a plum, pulling taut over whatever ridge or prominence you observed, and her features quite delicate, even exquisite. There was some wild strangeness to her hazel eyes.

"I wonder, were I a dog, which collar I'd choose."

"Yes. Well, as you see, we've several types." I lifted them, one by one, from the display-boxes for which placement on the counter drug salesmen vied, and whose garish and comic-strip trashiness suffused them, and their back-room marketing mentors, with religious joy and fulfillment. How they'd love to plant a hidden camera that they might later, in covert replay of images, discern some cryptic bit of intelligence about the mode and sequence of my fingerings, precious stuff to augment their spying demographics, to explain man's motivations, the workings of his very heart and soul. "These all murder fleas in their sleep, or at table. Ticks too, but not so well. Some of the ticks wake up later and mother future generations of pests." I thought of clients, gorging on blood (mine) and breeding more clients, as I winked in the direction of Sarah and Nick.

"He's very large. Very strong. He's wonderful protection." Her eyes seemed adrift over myriad subjects other than those her voice addressed.

"Yes. Aren't they all."

"Which would you choose if you lived with a dog like that?"

"I think this one." I proffered one from a box upon which my

102

desultory hand had come to rest. Let the marketing and advertising geniuses figure that one out.

"And why?"

"Good as another. Odor's not offensive." Sounded good. I was convinced.

"Why do they insist upon mounting one's leg?"

"Ah, it's sexual. A surrogation."

"Yes! I thought it. I would not have him neutered. Too many are. I hate the very idea."

"Would do no good against well-formed habits."

"My husband beats him, though. Men are so . . . Jealousy? He must know the nature of the act. Yes. I must ask him. I never have, you know. But then, you know him." She cast up and away the hand of exasperation.

I said nothing. I'd never laid knowing eyes on her husband. Nick played and sang a gentle and homey ballad, as if she weren't there. As everyone else in our town disregarded her, I supposed.

"Though, he's better protection than my husband. Perhaps it's time."

"For what?"

"No. It's time. What time does. My husband scarcely goes anywhere anymore. I bring him things, of course. His old favorites. Pipe tobacco and such. Well, this collar, then."

I took a large size, started to drop it into a brown bag.

"No, in here, if you please."

She spread the cloth bag by its handles. I hesitated, not sure I ought to thrust an insecticide-impregnated collar in a place where an exposed head of lettuce lay rusting, sleeping next to another derelict, a blighted orange, and an ancient tin of tobacco, a worn book, a faded package of condoms, and something else, crinkled and half-wrapped in waxed paper, like a bitten-into sandwich. And this only the top layer, the one I could clearly see.

I looked into her face. Nothing. I thrust the boxed collar in without a sense of direction.

"How, uh, how old is your dog?"

"Your records know all that. Do people ever look up what they file away? You know Bing. I've had the same dog for . . . for ever so many years. He's no smaller or larger. Protective. Very protective."

I had never laid eyes upon her dog, either, of that I was certain, for this day was my first for her, face-to-face. I knew her in the way everyone did. At a distance. Over her solitary coffee in a corner of the café; standing off to one side at an estate sale; at the nursery purchasing a plant, perhaps for her husband's pleasure at table; in the park, strolling, looking down, picking up; everywhere, but always within a capsule of solitude. Funny, how familiar, not to know anything of her, and always meaning to ask, yet never did I. But then, who would have known had I bothered? I decided to play it out to Nick's bluesy tune.

"I'm sorry, then, to have forgotten your name. But really, Mrs. . . ." she added nothing, " I don't believe I've ever seen your dog."

She looked at me with a blankness like balmy weather. Or opaquely, all power cut; an ice storm.

Dreamily, she asked: "Do they ever get over it? Get well again?"

"Who?"

"Any of them."

"Dogs? Is your dog . . . ?"

"Any of us. Over needing? The wretchedness it afflicts us with?"

Nick had stopped playing. Sarah applauded, fervently, and they fell into conversation while I stared at this enigmatic woman. Warily, they talked, their antennae up. I was sure they had heard all this.

"Any of us?"

"My husband will be in to pay you. When he can."

"Well . . . I don't . . . that's fine, but if you'd just refresh my memory. To note it in my records, you see."

Blank again.

"Your . . . his name?"

"What do they matter? No one remembers. Really, what do they? The festival begins soon, doesn't it? I love fairs and festivals. Do you?"

It was months away. In fall. I began to believe her a grifter.

"I need to put down something."

"There's life in them. Needs are met. More life than other gatherings—church services, funerals. Like that. Life's all we have, you know."

She plumped the crimson cloche, folded shut her bag, turned in a single flow of motion. "All we have," she said over her shoulder at the door, and departed.

Nick's darkly bearded face scrutinized mine, saw the questions therein. I noticed his hair was longish, but more cap than cape. Thick, though, dark, like his beard and his eyes.

"Do you know what existentialism means?"

I told him I thought I did.

"He also knows what charity means . . . and being soft," said Sarah, smiling, for she never held it against me.

"Fine line," Nick said, "between what the average person sees as borderline insanity and that. She may qualify. Either way, though I don't think she's insane. Or a con artist. Notice her eyes?"

"How not notice them?"

"Typical. Detached. No existentialist 'practices' anything. They just are, yet they're awed. That is, they exist but have difficulty being . . . and wonder why they exist . . . though how they exist, how they seem to anyone else, is their cinema of attitudes and actions . . . that may sound crazy itself. They dread, but they seek being, some of them, as the highest good. Look, I'm not fond of double-talk. Why do you do what you do?"

Though I felt I did not know him well enough, I was not troubled by that in his presence. There seemed to be no barriers to what one could address with this man, or his demeanor, his manner, wiped them away as meaningless, so I said it: "I'm trained for it."

"And that's all? That's why?"

"It's come to that. I'd appreciate the word not getting out."

He smiled, as if admonitions like that were, with him, absurdly unnecessary. "You are going to prove interesting, Doctor Lerner. Oh man, man, that feeling . . . I know that one, alright."

"Not . . . altogether, mind you. I'm reachable. I can be moved by people . . ."

"Yes. We've seen that."

"What's the word? Malleable. Yes. Rather be mutable."

He smiled. "Possibility that she's more attuned to life than you are. Something vaguely erotic about her. Does that bother you? Well, your admission was my own, was the reason I left."   .

"Left where?"

"Chicago. Industrial design."

105

"And now?"

"Whatever and wherever."

Sarah, still puzzling, said: "Erotic?"

"I said 'vaguely.' Just a perception."

"I see in her the sad buffoon," I said. "The sad circus lady in harlequin. No symmetry with the other, 'erotic.'"

"You're just uncomfortable with 'erotic.' Oh well, we arrive by different roads, yet we're all here together."

"Especially in your music. You play and sing extremely well."

"It's a hobby. It's what I do. It's something I do and never tire of, I should say."

"One or two I've never heard. The bluesy number."

"They're my own. I write some."

"Nick, it's not every day that a country veterinary clinic gets its own troubadour. That was really quite . . ."

"Oh, but I'm not 'your own.' I'm mine, for better or worse." He laughed engagingly. That magical openness again, an innocence no matter the number of roads: despite the roads. "I'm not sure I'm here for long, but I might be. I never know. Any notion where I might get a room?"

"The night? A week?"

"Something maybe in a home. Someone's home. Where it wouldn't matter about a night or a week."

Sarah piped up, made the offer. Nick accepted. I was glad, and dismissed the niggling thought he'd been wangling with a guitar for a lever.

The sixties were a decade cold, but Nick seemed to me an I, a holdover, a flower-child, though he was obviously too young to have been. He bespoke the issues, all right, but had not even the parentage, for from ultra-conservative parents he had fled. He'd go with me, seemingly fascinated, when I fed the cattle, morning and evening, or when I'd kill and pluck a couple of fryers, or gather in wood for the range we cooked upon, but not once did he lend a hand. And not that expected. He was our guest. His eyes cast dreamily about, gathered in nuance like traps.

I was so sure he missed nothing that I wished I could see the reassembled drama through his eyes . . . or see any drama at all to the

106

mundane and automatic things I did. When one of the girls answered back flippantly at table, he recorded, I could tell, especially our reactions to what they said or did. The baby calves playing at dusk, driving their dams into a frenzied and bawling chase of their own, each after her own offspring, Nick took in also, musing long upon the milling scene. I guess you'd say his entire manner and being were philosophic.

Nick told me, somewhat avidly, I thought, of recent work with something called "Acid Rescue," so I adduced that he'd made the obligatory pilgrimage of curious youth to its mecca in the west, that limp-letter-L-shaped seismic fracture of a state. Where else would they hold a telephonic ear to crisis? Not here, certainly. Or maybe an ear to the rail to detect the "vibrations" of chaos by the trainload, out there. No, not here, where denial reigned, or stoicism, or denial followed by stoicism once the consequences realized from the actions denied; or where unacknowledged unrest got pickled in alcohol. And Nick had knocked around at this and that: radio stations, vineyards, logging camps, and on construction crews that slashed aside forests for the paving of a black-paved way in for folks who'd destroyed what woodland peacefulness remained to them.

Or so he laughingly essayed it. You could tell he forgave them. His guitar and song had no doubt won him welcome in all these things, these places.

Within days, Nick found an abandoned farm house out from the north edge of town, and rented it with money from God-knows-what, whom, or where. I confess I was not saddened by his leaving, for he'd begun to haunt me like another spectator-self—or is it conscience? He saw too much, had done more in his few short years of vagabondage as to place my own bondage in harsh relief and new light. And I was already aware of it, the burgeoning futility of it all . . . all I did and could not do, all I did not avail myself of (too busy), all my failure to content myself with saving a few, easing it for more, and with a life of devotion to clients and that alone, since it had been my own choice.

I'd see him in passing. In town. As to some pied piper, a gaggle of obeisant and blasé kids from the high school matriculated wherever he held forth with words and guitar. Adults had begun to worry, I was told. Why not? Isn't that what adults do, I wondered? Town kids' cars had been collecting in the yard and all along the driveway and dooryard of his old house in the purlieus. Nearly every night the cars lay about at random, as if dropped there by a careless child at its sandbox.

Soon after, however, one of the more ardent kids was hospitalized. An overdose of something foreign to his parents. But then, the only thing not foreign to parents here is gossip and officiousness. For example, knowing he'd stayed with us gave them leave to make us officially aware of all their observations and suspicions concerning Nick. As if we were responsible, somehow.

And Nick? Why, he was the same ingenuous minstrel, working his way. He held no other job. Sometimes he'd drop in and play for us, and sometimes recite. His poetry was not bad at all, eclectic in influence as space-age life, metered but never rhymed. Fashionable. In some ways, perhaps, profound, though I found I could never again recall a word of it.

No one had anything to link with Nick the occurrence that had had plenty of precedent, if anyone forthright had deigned to admit it. Our dust-caked police busted someone every week with cannabis or hash, and sometimes more, though only they would admit of it. The weekly paper ignored it, the possessors having been townies.

Sarah asked, one night: "Matt, don't you . . . you don't think there's anything to it? You don't really believe all we're hearing, do you?" And I'd replied, "I try to remember his music. My feelings when I heard it. The poetry, I can't recall at all. But the music, I remember that. I felt all the better for it."

I, running the roads like my degree was no more than some hack operator's license, passed his place often.

"Looky there, Doc," said Jenks on one of those passages. "Unmarked."

It was so. They had him staked. Highway patrol.

"Oh, that ol' woman? Crazier'n a loon," said Omer Ainslee. An old-timer, and of him I'd finally asked her identity. "But why'd you pick me out t'ask?" he asked with narrowing eyes.

"You've been around and I know you. But why'd you say that? About her, I mean?"

"Well, course, tain't crazy, that coat she wears sun er shine. Nope, though some ones says it. Fer what keeps out winter's cold, keeps out summer's heat, y'know. Yep," and his jaw set up like a closed vault.

Omer, of course, was not crazy; not by the para-logic hereabout, for I'd heard the like before. He had only the rudiments of dementia, but don't we all?

"Why, then?"

"You ever talk to her?"

"Yes. In my clinic."

"Got somethin' fer her dog, then, didn't she?"

"It is, after all, a veterinary clinic."

"Thass so, but her dog ain't."

"Isn't a clinic?"

"Ain't! Ain't like in aught. And so ain't her hubby she chants about and warns off . . . when she does. Ain't a friendly, gossipin' soul, y'know. Died years ago, they did, hubby an' dog. She's all alone."

"Well," I said, too dumb-stricken to say more. "But then, look at it this way. A kind of immortality. We're not gone until forgotten. She and they just exist anachronistically. I mean, to her they still exist because they're always on her mind."

"Ain't natural," he said, looking at me obliquely.

"What is?"

"Well, yeah. Thass so. Whut is? But d'you eat garbage?"

"I know about that, too. What restaurants and markets toss out back isn't always garbage. Wilted, that's all, or stale."

"So some ones says. Don't make no neverminds. Don't make whut she does sensible, fer it could be spoilt."

"She looks healthy to me. Youthful, too, though she couldn't be very young."

"Seventy ain't young, thass so."

"Seventy?"

"If a day. How long you reckon I been a-kickin' round here? My daddy'n me both farmed with mules in th' Big Lick bottoms. I seen some strange things in my time. Strange."

"Damn. Seventy. Her skin is smooth as cream."

"An' red. She's red all over, like Ol' Nick's paradise. Inside, too.

109

Seen that too, I'd reckon. Eh? Didn't ye?"

I'd had enough than to ask about the last.

They got Nick that same week. The bloated old Chief of Police, Clarence Nobbs, twin to a warthog, held up the plastic bags for the paper's photographer—and writer and editor. Tableau. Front-page stuff, and not just the Slocum weekly. Too good. The county seat, Null, had a daily the story also made. The compound, like a fine-ground feed supplement pressed into a brick, was sent for laboratory analysis and Nick and two local boys remanded to the county jail at Null. The article said that Nick caved under pressure, took the raiders right to his cache: a hole in the deep, rich soil behind the half-fallen barn. The substance had been packed in plastic, sealed and piled in a lard can lined with more film, and a moisture-absorbent material scattered about among the packets. Very elaborate. Very accomplished. Arraignment was to be swift, and the confiscated stuff and laboratory reports would constitute state's evidence at time of trial.

Each paragraph throbbed with the prose of heroism among the tax-paid vigilants, more saga than journalism. High-grade stuff, too, the paper boasted, for no one seemed to have been poisoned. The police had a new echelon, a rebuilt and dust-free edifice, for they'd got them all just in time to avoid all the death and destruction sure to follow something apocalyptic as drugs.

"Nick. Nick, Nick! What the hell?"

"Listen, I wrote a new one. You're elected audience. My first visitor. Only. Fool liberal, your practice will suffer when word leaks out."

The song was a witty jailhouse blues. Listening, I was detachable again, by the otherwordliness of Nick's voice and eyes, his strange and inexplicable innocence, and by a nostalgia—for the prisoners who had suffered for no more than their difference, their refusal to be meek, to be subsumed by easy conformism, for free thinking redolent like a heady, contemporary scent, as if there were still possibility.

I never intended to ask about guilt or innocence.

"Are you all right? I mean, how are you treated?"

110

"Royally, Matt. Royally. Fame's the name of their game and I'm their ticket. Prisoner of the year. There's talk of a fellowship, you know. Seriously," he began, much deeper in voice, causing both of us to laugh, "seriously, all turkeys dine superbly before Thanksgiving, and I'm the bird upon which they, in turn, will stuff. Listen to this one."

"No! Don't sing again. Are you their bird?"

"Cordon bleu. But I'm going to pretend I didn't hear that as your private inquiry. I'm going to presume that you know me better than they do."

I lowered my eyes. "I appreciate that. Faux pas."

"I'll be . . ." He looked around, then whispered, "I'll be gone in a week." He nodded to emphasize the words.

"You mean you're . . . what, the file and bed sheet game?"

"Not my style. But on this, no more. How's the family?"

"They're . . . all fine. They send their best."

"You like riddles?"

"Hate them."

"Too bad. But here's one anyway: What's innocent as a lamb, but bright-red on the outside, and lives in a house like yours and mine, save for the fact it's a time bomb—that is, loaded."

"Not my house. Was yours loaded?"

"No. The lamb's. And that's all you get from me."

Ah, the chagrin after the headline a week later. The Chief, old Nobbs himself, roasted like the peanut he was. Highway patrol, as well. The bar of stuff they'd analyzed was pure, all right. Pure vegetable. Soybean, and all roasty-toasty brown, like their spirits.

He'd taken them to it not nearly so bowed as they thought by their cogent words bent upon his intimidation. As a ploy. He gave it up early into the raid. The real stuff? If any? In the walls; in their wistful dreams of glory. Who knew? The town was no more tainted, and no less, by Nick's sojourn. But I never saw Nick again.

They said some older man had picked him up upon acquittal. An attorney? The father who he'd told me had no more use for him? Who'd packed him off originally, and again and again; afraid of his taint, convinced he was incorrigible.

"Where you reckon he's gone to, Doc?" Jenks asked of me.

"Where did he come from, Jenks? Where do rarities like free minstrels come from?"

"Good question, Doc."

"Both. Yours and mine."

Two weeks later, three weeks dead, they found her. The lady in red. She'd been hacked to pieces, scattered about a gaunt woodland, a dry stream bed. I knew the place, spectral and forbidding, more for endings than beginnings, so it was fitting.

Nothing so heinous, so horrific, had ever been recorded before, and never since, in Yelton County.

"What a coat was that one, Doc. They ever find it?"

"No, Jenks. They didn't"

"Where'd she ever come up with such a one?"

"Her husband, Joseph."

"Joseph. That was her . . ."

"The one with the coat of many colors. Hers was his bequest, he's dead you know."

Some joke, Jenks gave me to know by his scathing glance.

"I know. Tried to be facetious, but it's callous. But you know no one in town to this day ever knew her. No one took her for anything but granted. Don't you find that strange in the very garden of officiousness and brother's-keeper judgments?"

"Busybodies ain't Samaritans, Doc. You know that."

I did not tell him that callousness helps to relieve burdens. The evening before, I'd stopped when I saw the truck with the hoist parked toward the back of the town cemetery. No cars anywhere. No people gathered. No cenotaph, so I knew I was right. A concrete crypt was being lowered into the yawning earth, so I pulled in.

Then I saw him. Not the preacher. Standing near the grave, his hands folded, stood old Omer Ainslee. He looked to be praying.

I got out of the cab, quietly, tried to do the same. I hadn't been able to do it in too many years. I couldn't now. So I murmured softly: "Goodbye, old girl. Life's all we have. Let's hope there's something better—maybe fresher food," then got back in and drove before Omer could see that I'd seen him. No sense two of us being discomfited by our tears.

At the entrance to the cemetery, the sergeant of police, whose

dog I knew, hailed me. He's the one who filled in for me all details of
the crime scene, earlier. And something else, now. There were real
drugs. They knew that, now. The drugs were in her house. A
basement bin where she'd kept winter's tubers, and hidden among
some old and spewed jars of canning.

"She . . . she dealt in drugs," I blurted, incredulous.

"Wal, mebbe. Likely not."

"Well, then . . ."

"That hippie. That boy you known. Stayed with ye, didn't he?
Lived not half a mile through them woods from her—them woods
where we found 'er. It's a riddle, ain't it? Sight on earth, an' him
runnin' free."

"Yes. Free," I said, "yes, and a riddle," recalling now.

"We'll get the bugger. Got out a APB."

"You know the real drugs were his?"

"Got fingerprints that match on the jars."

"He's no killer. Not a chance in the world."

"Didn't say 'e was. They's other prints. Any o' these townie kids
that frequented th' place could of done it, that hung with th' hippie
boy. Fer th' drugs. But they didn't, neither, we don't think."

"Then . . . who?"

"I think you couldn't he'p but seen 'im jist now. I'm goin' back
in t'pick 'im up. Got 'is prints. On a axe."

"Who?"

"Oney one ever known 'er. Frequented 'er place, so it's said.
Look at 'im back in there in a overcoat, an' it plumb hot. Crazy as
her. Got here in th' nick of time, I'd say."

"Wouldn't *human* be a given?"

Escape from Amon-Tayol
Jodi Ralston

"Retrieve for me the Jewel of Amon-tayol," the wizard had said, *"and you shall be richly rewarded."* Standing at the verge of a dark and dead wood—something the wizard had neglected to mention—Rhyder wished he'd revised his opinion of desperateness *before* he'd embarked on this misbegotten "quest." Desperate men do desperate things, but he wondered how much he really needed to be "richly rewarded."

He eyed the direction that he'd come from and considered going back. Surely, knowledge of what lay before future seekers would be worth, perhaps, a small bag of silver? Then, he wondered exactly how many other seekers—perhaps, "suckers" was more apt—stood on this very spot, contemplating the very same thing. How many actually turned back? He knew the answer to how many had returned through the wizard's portal: none. Or perhaps, they *did* return, abandoning the quest, and the wizard had decided not to appreciate failure. He certainly didn't trust that beady-eyed man, not even with the key to the latrine.

With a hearty sigh, Rhyder swung his gaze back to the black, rotten forest before him, then checked the little magic hourglass he'd been given; the liquid-sands ran red, marking Day One, but displayed one-third empty. He'd have nigh on three days.

On a whim, he flipped the time-piece upside down, and upon seeing the sands now trickling skyward, quickly pocketed it. There were already enough oddities about due to magic. There was the dark wood, which even the rays of the burning sun could not seem to penetrate. Not to mention, he'd left behind a wizard's private workroom for this freaky land just by walking through a magical doorway. Rhyder gave a shudder, not looking forward to the trip home—that was, if he survived that long. And likely, he would need these magic trinkets for that, no matter how much he distrusted such things.

He regarded the wood one final, long moment, before shrugging. "Like there's anywhere else to look for His Greediness' Jewel, anyways." With that decided, he stepped through the blighted trees and into chill darkness.

* * *

Rhyder rested against a tree trunk he'd found—rather, smacked headfirst into—and counted by touch the bumps and scrapes he'd gained by bumbling through Deadwood. That was the most cheerful name he could think of for this place; Darkwood had come a close second.

Upon those thoughts, he pulled out the time-piece and wished heartily that it could burn away some of the darkness. The magic trinket was little better than a firefly's light to guide a man's way in a cloud-swallowed, moonless night. However, it *did* perform its one duty well: it glowed a baleful red, but only half-full—twelve hours spent, and twelve hours left until the new day trickled in green.

Traveling in pitch-blackness was tiring—and painful—work, he thought, as he returned to testing the tenderness of his nose for breakage. *Just sore; great, first luck o' the day.* And he decided to celebrate by taking a break. After all, he'd spent most of the day trekking through hot sunlight, then this dreadful darkness, with only the skimpiest fare for meals—thanks to a damn cheapskate wizard. In fact, he'd say he deserved a wee bit of shut-eye for all his efforts.

Wait, strike that; didn't Ol' Squints say, "sleep not." Well, hey, what's he know? He didn't think to mention this here wood or anything. No, indeed. Greedy ol' bugger, Rhyder decided. *Just wants his goods quick, I say. Too scared to come here himself and fetch his damn Jewel of Amok-whatever—or to even have a peek, to help his "seekers" quest for him.*

Thus decided, he tucked his time-piece away, leant back against the tree, and slept.

Rhyder woke when time ran green—with one-fourth wasted—and he cursed himself for being a lazy lout, sleeping away half the day. Then an odd thought niggled as he secured the timepiece: what had woken him, anyway?

Something cool brushed against the back of his hand. "So, you're awake now?"

"Sweet damn!" He jolted upright and away from the soft-spoken voice, and promptly smacked his head on a large limb overhead. "Ow, dammit!"

"That's a pretty magic-bauble. May I see it? We don't get much light, or visitors bearing magic, or, well, visitors at all in here."

"Oh, yeah?" Rhyder fumbled for his knife blade. "That right? Don't get out much, eh?"

"No, not really. Not if I care for my safety."

Rhyder flinched as the fingers found him again. God, at least he hoped they were fingers, and not some—*twisted*—thing else.

"Is this what you seek?" The press of hard steel against his gut froze Rhyder stiffer than an ice sculpture. "Well?"

"What d'you want?" Rhyder growled.

"To talk. The others always ran away when they'd heard me, or they'd never sleep. You actually slept."

"Lucky me," Rhyder gritted out. "Look, chap, I'm not the conversin' sort—" The blade pressed harder. "—but I could try."

"Excellent." The blade eased away from slicing him a new mouth. "Sit down, please."

Polite bugger, he thought, arching an eyebrow. Then, he realized his captor probably couldn't see the gesture anyway and gave it up.

Rhyder sat down, carefully. The other's fingers followed, creeping up his sides and aiming for his face. "Hey!" Rhyder squirmed, but didn't dare move away. "I'm not the, uh, touchy-feely sort, you know."

The other ignored this. If not for instinct, the cool questing, fingers might have scraped Rhyder's eyes. Instead, they skimmed over his eyelids, then lingered on the middle of his forehead. With a sigh, the cool touch retracted, and the captor said, "Have you come to relieve me of this place, stranger?"

"Uh, no, not exactly; I've come to relieve *something* from here. Didn't exactly expect *you*, though . . ."

"Elaborate, please."

"Some stone or gem. Wizard wants it."

"*That's* what you risk your life to seek? An absent wizard's stone? No." A colder, more dreadful touch than the captor's fingers lifted Rhyder's chin—the blade. "There must be more than you say. Lie not, stranger, for I can read you clearer than you might think."

"Then you must be blind, chap." He grunted as the knife pricked his throat. "I speak the truth! The wizard wants a Jewel of A-man-tail or whatnot."

The pressure eased suddenly. "Amon-tayol?"

"Yes, that's it."

"The wizard's name, quick!"

Damn. As if I know it! Rhyder sucked in a deep breath, mentally cursing himself—and the wizard—for landing him in this fix. He'd better do something, before he became skewered. "Look. Before you get quick with the blade—my own blade, might I add, and one I'd be liking back eventually—"

"You can retrieve it from your own hide, if you continue to dodge my question."

All right, delaying: not such a good idea after all. "Hey, do you see me dodging anything? Like I was saying, I can't give it."

The other sighed, as if he dealt with a trying child. "Now, my friend, I wish to make this painless as possible."

"Nice to know; painlessness is always a nice, uh, touch to gaining and keeping friends," Rhyder said.

"Then, *friend*, give me his name—I shan't ask again." The knife blade pressed snug against his skin. "Mind the truth, or I'll start poking you full of holes. Your choice, but make it quick!"

"I've been saying! I'd be happy to give it as a token of our, uh, budding friendship, but I can't." As Rhyder was getting mighty tired of being threatened by his own weapon, he reached out and restrained a cool wrist—or so he hoped. "But, I can't give it t' ya, 'cause *I don't know it to give.*"

"He never gave you his name?" The voice sounded surprised. "His seeker in this place?"

"Never. You can stand a vow by that." Then he decided it was time to ask a question of his own, before his captor-friend got too disappointed. Disappointed strangelings, after all, were a dangerous sort. "*What* are you?" He released the wrist, careful to stay away, as best as possible, from what it held. "Human?"

"Yesss . . . you might say that."

That did *not* sound real encouraging. "Might, eh? Either you are, or you ain't."

"What does it matter to you?" Now, whatever it was didn't sound so much peevish as tired and discouraged.

"Look, chap," Rhyder said, "I know if I were questioning my human-ness, I'd say that warrants speaking of, that's all. And from

118

what I suppose, you've not had many chances with my fellow seekers."

"Are you offering," the speaker asked, "to stay and be my
companion?"

Oh, nice hole, Rhyder; dug that yourself, eh? Why not try for a
little deeper. Aloud, he said, "Uh, no, that is, uh—no, not exactly."

The other sighed—again—and then pressed something into his
palm. Rhyder flinched, expecting to be stabbed, bewitched, or have
the life sucked from him, as that all sounded like proper doings for a
ticked off evil being.

But his captor merely said," Then there's naught of which to
speak. You are free to go, stranger. I've returned your blade."

So the creature had. Slowly, carefully Rhyder rose to his feet.
Then a curious thought struck him. "What good would a wizard's
name do ya, anyways?"

Surprisingly, his former captor answered, "I could command
him to release me from my exile."

"What?" Rhyder shook his head. "Anyway, you sure that's the
only way outta here?"

Silence.

It had better not be the only way. He damn sure didn't fancy
being stuck here too. He fought a shiver as another terrible dread
struck him. "There's no stone, is there?"

"Naught but naught resides here. No magic artifacts, no
treasure; only a dead forest and a blighted land of light."

Something didn't make sense. Where were all his predecessors?
Surely, Squints wasn't punishing them for failure by leaving them
here. And why would Squints send seekers anyway, if nothing were
here? He mulled this over a moment before asking, "Why did the
others never return?"

"They most likely died. There's a demon that prowls this
Realm."

"Oh. *Really*? Somehow, I don't count that as nothin', ya know."

The other did not reply.

"Look," Rhyder said. "I had a reason for bringing this up."

"Hmm. Really? One couldn't tell by your sense of direction: you
always seem to lose track of the point."

"Ha, ha. Well, then, maybe I won't offer you a way out."

"What!" Rhyder heard a rustling—the first noise the other made, beyond his voice. Then, his shoulders were grasped. "You know of a way out? But you said your wizard withheld his name. How?"

"Oh, aye, not a name, but just as good. The wizard, he gave me a deadline. He aims to retrieve me."

Rhyder paused a moment, to quickly contemplate the insanity of this proposition. He decided to damn with it, and said, "Look here, as I see it, we need each other. I have no Amonny—"

"Amon-tayol—"

"Yeah, yeah, what I said—no *stone* to fetch, and I don't want to share the fate of my fellow seekers, get me?"

"You want my aid in returning to the Land of the Light unscathed. And in exchange, you'll take me with you when your wizard calls?"

"Yeah, bright chap you are. So, we dealing, or no?"

"Won't he notice you have naught for him?"

"Hey, we have plenty o' . . ." At that reminder, Rhyder took out his time-piece: the green was cut in half. He shook it, hard. "I knew it—I knew I didn't sleep twelve hours straight! Damn wizard crap! Don't work right; never should've put trust in it."

"Oh, don't!" The cold fingers reached for the glowing trinket. "You don't know how precious such light, such magic is!" And the creature cradled the time-piece in his hands as if it were a newborn babe the midwife had just laid into a father's arms.

"Uh, yeah," Rhyder said. He nudged his newfound guide forward and followed in his wake. "You keep a hold o' that for me. Great."

And without warning, he bumped into the stilled creature—it felt as hard as stone. Before he could back away, cool fingers gripped his arm—in camaraderie this time. And the voice was its softest yet: "Thank you, I'll treasure it forever."

"Yeah, well, if you think a day's forever, sure. Now, let's move on out."

After some groping and tromping through the dark wood, Rhyder asked, "So, what's with the touchy-grabby stuff back there?"

"Pardon?"

120

"Grabbed my face, scared the willies outta me, remember?"

"Oh. I had to be sure of what you were."

"Wouldn't *human* be a given?"

"I had to be certain—I never managed to talk with any . . . visitors before. I wasn't sure if you *weren't* a wizard. On the forehead," the other explained, "a wizard bears a mark either detectable by sight or touch."

"By sight or touch, huh?" He looked about him, at the absolute nothingness darker than a night without moon or stars, darker than a nightmare that gobbled up such things, and decided it prudent to not think deeply on that. Instead, he asked, "And the eyes?"

"To see if you were a demon."

Now, *that* intrigued him. "How's that?" Curious that a strangeling would worry about another strangeling.

"Demons don't have eyelids."

He'd had to touch Rhyder to find out. "So you can't see in the dark?"

"No, not completely. I see faint shapes at times. Everything that doesn't naturally belong in the wood is lighter than the surroundings."

"Well, that's funny. *You* don't seem lighter, any."

"To your eyes . . . ? No, I would not."

Oh, that was helpful . . . and creepy. The rest of the moment passed in silence, and Rhyder suddenly wished he hadn't parted with the time-piece. At least, he'd know how time ran then. If he didn't get to the designated place all punctual-like, the wizard would leave him here with Deadwood, Demon, and Strangeling for companionship. Not his idea of fun.

Speaking of the Squints . . . "So, our plan: we need one. What's precious here in A-monkey-tails, anyway?"

"There's naught. Just deadness and dread."

"Ah," Rhyder said. "Nothing? Well, didn't think it would be *that* easy, no." He sighed expressively through his nose. "So, what *is* A-m—"

"The word you mangle? *Amon-tayol.* And it's where you stand."

Rhyder held up and looked toward ground, half-expecting to see something special through the darkness.

The other laughed, like water trickling over stones in a fountain;

it was a strange and unexpected laugh. "No, silly one. Do you not know what Realms are? They are magical worlds beyond the one you call home, accessed only by wizards. This Realm, this magical world, bears the name Amon-tayol."

"Ah." Now, Rhyder understood. And until now, he hadn't even a notion that this wasn't home anymore—suspected himself in some strange land he'd never heard of, maybe, but a whole other world just brimful of magic? That would almost seem too incredible if he hadn't seen what he'd seen, heard what he'd heard. But damn all, he wished *someone* might have explained some of this *earlier*. After all, it probably would've been just a wee bit helpful for a treasure-seeker to know, wouldn't it?

He gave a disgusted sigh. "So, all this is Amon—"

"—Tayol, yes. Its name bears some significance, as all names do, but this is a Forgotten Realm, known only to a few. I doubt any survived to know its origin; though, there is quite some speculation on that matter . . ."

Great. Not only was he *really, incredibly* far away from home, but likely, he was in a world forgotten by everyone save Squints and Strangeling here.

". . . then again, it might not have always looked like this. So the name could have been descriptive of something besides the present, gross variances in land and—"

"Say—" He interrupted what felt like could be a very long-winded spiel; something that might be interesting to his companion, but didn't seem to be particularly helpful in getting them the damn out of this place. Now, learning something about his companion of this world might just be. It was something anyway. "Say, friend, while we're on names, do *you* have one?"

"Do you?"

"A name? Sure. Rhyder—" He gave his best impression of a courtly bow, though he wondered how well his companion could rightly appreciate it. "At your service, oh benighted one."

A light touch fell on his arm, as cautioning as the voice. "You should guard your name more closely. It grants wizards especial access, and that is fearful power in the wrong hands." There was a pause, then: "Names are such intimate things, as I was explaining before. But—" The strangeling took a deep breath. "I am . . . I am

Leall."

Leall laughed suddenly, a noise of mingled relief and delight. "Oh, I have not used that name in a long time. It feels . . . good. As good as having someone with whom to talk."

As the other fell silent, Rhyder felt it prudent to change the topic. "So, this wizard: what'll we give him? Just a plain, garden-variety rock? That won't work, see—he's a crafty sort. Beady-eyes an' all that. He's gonna sniff out our trick as soon as we're through the portal."

"That won't be the problem. No, the hard part, my friend, will be getting him to open another portal so soon after the last."

Rhyder ran a hand through his hair. "I don't see . . ."

"Portal-opening takes great magic—and, consequently, drains greatly. Only a wizard's magic protects him from mortal weapons. Although he possesses strong vision under ordinary circumstances, the strain to hold the passage will take great concentration, especially after opening one just days ago. Moreover, I hope—I *believe*—greed shall color his perception."

Ah, now Rhyder understood. "How'd you get so wizard-wise?"

"Still a moment!"

Rhyder did, though wondering why.

Then, the answer came: "Behold, Friend Rhyder; before you: daylight!"

It was all that Leall said and more. The faintest slivers of light, a promise of relief, shattered the world of blackness. Beacons of salvation. How Rhyder could be so distracted by chatter as to miss such a heartwarming sight as this, he did not know. And he no longer cared, either. He rushed forward, eager to be shed of the darkness' heavy touch.

And he was brought up short by a firm command: "Wait!"

Rhyder was hard put to, but he did as bidden, standing on the verge of the wood. He was only a step away from shedding the disturbing darkness for refreshing light. So close . . .

"I must follow you, but I want you to . . ." Leall took a deep, shaky breath. "I—I want you to brace yourself, Rhyder. As I told you before, I am not—quite—human."

Rhyder nodded. "Uh, all right." He stepped backwards, into the open, lighted plain, keeping an eye on his companion's general vicinity.

After a moment's hesitation, Leall followed—and Rhyder got his first look at the company he kept.

"Sweet-God-o'-Mercy!"

When Leall had said he wasn't *quite* human, he was correct. In nearly every aspect save one, he looked like a young, male human, but it was the single exception that seemed so . . . creepy.

Leall was made entirely of silver-grey *stone*.

And Leall stood still, so still, like a living statue, that Rhyder found himself instinctually backing away. Only when he nearly fell onto his ass, tripping over a fallen log, did he stop and gain hold over himself.

And only then did Leall speak, "Rhyder, I wasn't always as you see me before you."

"Uh . . ."

Then stone-boy lifted his chin and stated proudly, "Once, I too was a great wizard." If he could have swirled his robe or swished back his straight, shoulder-length hair, Leall looked as if he would have, something that reminded Rhyder distinctly of Squints. Yet not. It was pride, he reasoned, like any wizard he'd seen possessed—but not arrogance like in Squints.

And if he had to pick whose company he'd keep, he'd pick stone-boy over Squints any day. After all, Leall had guided him all this way and let him in on the truth of this land. Now, Squints had—well, Squints had just plunked him down, leaving him blind as a bat to boot in the ways that mattered. Not to mention, he knew exactly what he'd meant to Squints: A means to an end; seeker number, what? Ten? Twenty? He doubted Squints even kept track.

The sensation of creepiness began to seep from him at this reasoning. After all, Leall hadn't changed, only the ability to see Leall had.

And at the moment, he could see a frown marring the stony-façade. He'd better say something, quick. "I, uh, see you have a . . ." Rhyder pointed to his own forehead. "Thing." He spoke the truth; there was a blue dot amiss with the rest of the multi-hued grey. But he grimaced. *What, couldn't think of anything more lame?*

But Leall just nodded. "My wizard's mark."

Curious. Squints' was red. An ugly red at that, like anything was appealing about the fellow. But Rhyder decided not to question that, having a feeling he'd be listening to a long spiel on magicky stuff well above his head and beyond his interest.

Leall took a hesitant step forward, eyeing Rhyder speculatively. When Rhyder didn't react, the chap's stone lips pulled into a smile. "Wonderful. We make no progress if you fear me. Come, friend, let's walk as we talk, for we lose time."

"Ah . . . oh, right-o."

Rhyder turned and let Leall fall into step beside him. Then he noticed another oddity: though made of stone, the chap made not a single sound as he walked. That aspect definitely reminded him of the other wizard, Squints. To himself, Rhyder muttered, "Definitely a wizard-chap. Yup."

"You're probably wondering how I came to be here and in this form."

Rhyder was.

Leall continued. "I journeyed through a portal, one I opened myself—a mistake. For it rendered me thus."

"So that's why the ol' goat won't set foot here himself!"

"Yes. I was young and full of more ambition than fair sense, and I thought it—" Leall waved a hand to encompass his living-stone body. "—a mere tale to keep treasure-seekers away. I was wrong, evidently."

Leall shrugged his shoulders, and Rhyder realized he was listening and watching for signs that Leall showed properties of his otherworldly nature. Yet, no crackling heralded any breakage; equally nonexistent were sounds of brushing and settling stone against stone. And he'd already noticed that Leall walked as silently as a wizard. Must be some wizard-stone, Rhyder decided, and left it at that.

He realized Leall was regarding him with a questioning look, and he hastened to cover his open staring. "Say, Leall, can you, de—uh—stone yourself once you get back?"

"Oh, I dearly hope so! But to be free of this Realm, that would be wish granted enough for me."

"Ah, well, as for me, I'd aim higher."

Leall's eyes, akin to sparkling blue jewel-studs, slid his way. A smile carved upward curves on the stony face. "Truly now? Tell me this, Rhyder: what did the wizard promise you?"

Jewels and gold coins danced before Rhyder's eyes, happily blotting out the dreary landscape. He smiled as he said, "Great riches."

Laughter erupted again, reminiscent of a bubbling brook over a stony bed. "I'm afraid you've been tricked, my friend. *You shall be richly rewarded.'* " Leall laughed again. "That usually translates to: you can keep your life as payment; that is more than reward enough for daring to deal with wizards!"

Rhyder clenched his fists hard. "I'm gonna crush that beady-eyed fork-tongue like the bug he is!"

"Wait, my friend." Leall laid a hand upon his forearm. "Before you act so hastily, I wish you to know this: you *will* receive a great reward." Only when Rhyder stopped did Leall continue. "You shall be my companion."

Rhyder even felt his brow furrow with his confusion. "Uhm, not to sound ungrateful . . ."

Leall smiled and said, "Scantly known is this among commoners, but a wizard's companion is held in high prestige—and more importantly, I assume, to you is this: he wants for naught that his wizard can provide." Leall cocked his head slightly, seeking a better way to explain. "You are a sort of champion. As kings are fond of champions, so are wizards. Everyone wants a hero to claim."

"But I'm no hero—and certainly, I ain't good at protecting and sword-fighting stuff."

"I wouldn't expect you to be. Ours are not necessarily weapon-savvy champions, as such. A wizard's companion is anyone whom we take in interest in, someone to keep us in touch with the common world. You're only expected to be a trustworthy, loyal familiar—*a friend.*" Leall looked away with a sigh, then continued. "Being so elevated above common man's reach is a lonely position within to reside. And wizards are too rivalrous to make true friends amongst our caste." Again, the jewel-eyes regarded Rhyder. "Besides, to me, as my rescuer from this fiendish prison, you *are* a hero."

It seemed simple enough. Be Leall's friend and live a life crammed full of luxury. Oh, he could do that, easily. "Well, you've got yourself a companion, then, chap."

They shook on it before continuing their trek across the bleak, rolling plain.

* * *

Rhyder snatched a fist-sized, roundish, odd-looking stone from atop a sun-bleached tussock and proceeded to toss it up in the air and catch it. "The makings of a wizzy Jewel." He turned towards his wizard. "Say, Leall, what time—"

A loud crack startled him, causing him to drop his stone. Damn all, he thought. Just what we don't need right now: a storm. He looked behind and skyward for traitorous clouds, but the sky showed clear of all but the burning sun. "What the—?"

The booming noise repeated. Now that he really listened, it reminded him less and less of anything as normal as a thunderstorm. Rather, it sounded like something large and determined was making its way through something equally determined to remain just where it was. And it seemed the first party was winning: black treetops in the heart of Deadwood shook and waved like tall prairie-grass in a sharp wind, as another crash beat out from the forest—breaking timber. Rhyder stared numbly at the awesome sight, at the quiver running through the tall, massive trees.

"Oh, no—the beast!" Leall clapped a hand on Rhyder's forearm and jerked.

But he couldn't quit staring, awaiting a glimpse of what could wreak that amount of damage.

"Rhyder, we must hasten onwards!" And Leall started pulling.

"Holy . . ." Rhyder shook his head hard. He was trembling as he turned away from the woods and the dark swath being cut within.

Still, the destructive din continued relentlessly, seeming to pick up speed as his feet finally got the hint to start moving. "God! How'd you escape *that*?" He flung his arm back in the direction of the woods.

At a very large crash, he couldn't resist temptation. He looked back: a mistake. The beast had pushed beyond the halfway mark. He felt his body down to his feet begin to leaden again; he slowed, gaping.

"You don't," Leall answered. "You stand very still and pray very hard, instead. As I'm the only one who currently resembles a statue, I suggest calling out your wizard. Now! We are close enough to your point of arrival."

"G-good idea; what's a few miles here and there to a wizard, eh?

I'll just—no, damn, wait!" He hauled back down the hill to retrieve his nearly forgotten rock. "Need a Jewel, remember? 'Fraid you just won't work, chap."

"He won't be deceived by that!"

An idea came to him, and he said, "The time-thingy, give it."

Blinking, Leall extended his closed fist. The fingers uncurled slowly, exposing the hourglass—two-thirds full and blue. "What good—?"

Rhyder snatched it from the palm, and smashed it against his round stone.

"No!" The other rushed forward too late to save it, and Rhyder proceeded to smear the sticky, gritty liquid all over the makeshift Jewel.

"Perfecto." He pushed the "Jewel" into Leall's hands. "Hold this and make like a statue."

"What a waste," Leall said, his voice soft and whiny as he gazed upon the stone.

"Statue, Leall. Wait, no, hide your blue-spot." Rhyder lifted Leall's hands up to press against his wizard-marked forehead. Now, Leall looked as if he were praying while clasping something blue-glowing and precious. That looked suitably arcane and wizard-like to Rhyder.

Rhyder smiled and patted Leall on the back. "And if it gets us outta 'ere, I don't call it a waste, get me?"

"Let's just hope you are right."

"Let's." He turned towards the far too-open vista before him and bellowed, "Sir Wizard, it is I, your Seeker, Rhyder!" As he waited—and prayed—for a response to the predetermined words, he couldn't help but look askance at their danger.

Now, the black trees splintered and toppled near the very verge they'd escaped from earlier. Within bare moments, the beast would be on the plain, in prime hunting lands. And they would be sitting ducks.

"Seeker Rhyder?"

At the booming voice, he nearly fell down the hill. As once before, a great blue rectangle hovered, shimmering in the air. But now it felt too narrow and cramped despite the fact that the portal stretched twice his own height and was wide enough to fit his breadth. No doubt it was all the same as before, save for one marked difference: a giant eyeball floated at the top of the portal, taking up the full width.

"You are . . ." The eye narrowed in suspicion. "Early." It lowered to the middle of the doorway, barring the way through. "For what reason am I called?"

A final, splintering crack told Rhyder the beast had made its way through the woods. He fought against body-quaking trembles, as he hooked his thumb rearward. "Yeah, uh, had some unexpected company, sir."

The eye bobbed back up and peered beyond him, squinting as if it needed glasses. Then, several dreadful heartbeats later, the eye widened.

"Sir!"

It flicked back downwards, fixing him with a gimlet stare. "Did you succeed?"

He barely had time to nod before its gaze snapped in every-which direction, searching.

"Where is it!"

Then, it spotted his companion, and Rhyder prayed Leall was doing a fair statue impression. After all, a moving one would be quite suspect.

"Fool! Do you think a wizard of my eminence and sagacity as a simpleton?" The eye flared at him, the pupil burning hot-coal-red now. "That is *not* the Jewel!" The portal flickered alarmingly, as if about to fade away into thin air and leave them stranded.

"Sir, please! Wait!"

The flickering stopped. "Speak quickly."

"Your grandship, sir! I have it—well, rightly, *he* has it." He jerked his thumb toward Leall. "I, uh, just can't loose it, sir. No time to, see."

While the eye squinted at Leall, Rhyder peeked over his shoulder and felt the blood drain from his face.

The creature—a slathering, black hulk—fastened burning, lidless red eyes upon him. The mouth that made up half the demon's body was full of gnashing teeth, teeth heavily serrated and nearly thrice the length of Rhyder's arm. That mouth worked open and closed, open and closed, as if the demon imagined munching on him, and the loosed groan told him it liked what it imagined very well.

As it lurched up the hill, the demon looked—and smelled—like a dung-heap bred with a giant slug. And like a slug, it left behind a slime-trail—but one that rotted and bubbled the land in its wake. Two thick tentacles writhed, striving for him, as if screaming "Gimme, gimme."

Rhyder whirled back. "God! Sir, *please!*"

The eye blinked at him, a tad sluggishly. The gaze flicked behind him before its owner's voice intoned at long last, "Proceed."

As soon as the bobbing eye faded from existence, Rhyder picked up statue-Leall—and nearly dropped him in surprise. He grunted. "Lightweight you ain't!"

But a far-too close growl helped hasten him along; he had them both heaved through the portal in no time.

A howl of loss shivered through the marrow of his bones. Then, he was blind and deaf, aware of nothing but a persistent tugging—the glorious magic bringing him safe and home.

Rhyder set down Leall with a resounding clap, earning him a quick glare before the eyes closed again. Fortunately, Squints was too busy closing the portal to pay them any attention. It gave him time to catch his breath and scattered senses. Then it was time to get down to business, for the portal was gone, faded away to nothingness. Rhyder cleared his throat noisily.

And Squints ignored him, fishing through some scattered items on a tabletop.

Just when Rhyder considered simply sneaking Leall and himself away, Squints turned on them, with talon-like fingers clenching a long metal spike and a hand mallet. The leer he gave Leall made Rhyder's stomach twist with disgust, and he wished he could just pummel on the man for a while.

"Uh, sir," he said, softening his tone with meekness. He stepped forward, hand surreptitiously fingering for his knife. "You mentioned a reward?"

Annoyance flickered over the greed-set features before Squints waved him away, as if flicking aside a nagging fly. Then, attention fastened wholly upon Leall's hands, Squints stalked forward step by slinky step.

"No, sir," Rhyder said, dropping the subservient tone. With a flash of steel, he had the blade at the man's ribcage. "I think you'll dismiss me not." The wizard froze.

"How dare you!" Squints dropped his weapons, and fixed Rhyder with a venomous glare. "You'll pay for this with your life!"

"Again . . . no." He jerked his head towards the table. "Friend, see if you can't find some trussing things, eh?"

Squints' head jerked around so swiftly that Rhyder thought—hoped—the wizard popped a neck bone.

Smiling now, Leall tossed aside the fake-Jewel with a loud clatter. "Of course."

"Impossible!" Then arrogance replaced the brief surprise. "You dared to deceive me? A wizard of my powers!"

"Dared and done, *Your Eminence*. And quite easily at that."

Shortly, they had the wizard bound. Even as they "guided" Squints to a handy chair and strapped him in, the threats flew. "Once I am free, you'll wish to God that you were never born. You'll beg that I leave you to the tender mercies of the smime-mmfer!" The rest of the words were cut short, as Leall thrust a wad of cloth in Squints' mouth, securing it with a long strip from the wizard's blue silk robe.

"There, one mustn't forget the gag when trammeling a wizard."

"Duly noted, my wizard."

"Ah, I feel more like my old self already!" Indeed, the grey stone seemed to mute and shift. Hues were seeping out, exposing pale skin, bronze-blonde hair, and green, luxuriant robes.

Speaking of stones . . . Rhyder eyed the discarded fake-Jewel, which had left a bright blue smear on the pale-gold carpet. He smiled briefly at that. "You know, something's been tickling my mind," he said, while returning his knife to its leather sheath. "That time-oddity in the wood? I'm no wizard, but that seems awfully magicky to me, speeding time along like that."

Leall lifted his eyes from the staring match he'd engaged in with Squints. "So, you think that the Jewel *is* real? And in that wood? Because of the time distortion?"

"Well." Rhyder shrugged, then gestured for his wizard to start their departure. "It was . . . odd-like." Then again, that whole place wasn't exactly right as rain.

"I must admit," Leall said, while walking backwards towards the door, eyes fastened upon him. "I've never explored that region in its entirety."

"What'd ya do there: play roost for the birdies?" He reached out and nudged Leall a little, so the unaware wizard avoided smacking into the doorframe. "Hmm," Rhyder said to himself, pulling back his hand and flexing it. "Warmer already—and you're getting your color back right swift."

"Thanks." Leall fixed him with a halfhearted glare. "And I'll have you know, I was attempting to stay uneaten with a voracious beast constantly breathing down my neck, all the while seeking a way home. So, my companion, I wasn't lazing about, twiddling my thumbs, now was I?"

"All right, all right. But say, can you *attempt* to walk like a good lad?" Leall shrugged and complied. "Ah, there you go."

"But concerning your plan, I can see definite possibilities therein!" Ambling down the long, ostentatious hallway, Leall ran a speculative look over Rhyder. "Definite possibilities, indeed, my friend."

"Oh, no!" Rhyder cut the air sharply with both hands. "No, no, no! I'm no hero—and I've enough o' treasure-seekin'! Just forget I ever mentioned it!"

"But consider it, Rhyder: unforeseen magic potentials, the Jewel—and perhaps riches beyond belief for *you*. All just hidden deep within the wood!"

"I have. They pale next to death, death, oh, and did I mention? Death. Remember Slimy? Hankering for some human-chomping?"

But Leall's mind had journeyed elsewhere, already planning the return. "Oh, of course. First, we must slay the demon . . ."

Rhyder stifled a groan. Perhaps he should reconsider this so-called reward. Somehow, he doubted being Leall's companion would be the life of sloth and indulgence he so rightly deserved.

He hated so much that it actually scared him.

A WISE BOY ON A SNOWY NIGHT
Emily Spreng Lowery

Ellen set the table for breakfast that morning as if everything were normal. She put out four sky blue plates on creamy cotton place mats with stitched violets on the edges. She arranged four stainless steel sets of Pottery Barn flatware on top of cloth napkins folded into neat triangles and then set four tall orange juice glasses above the forks. Her throat was dry and eyes were bloodshot from lying awake almost all night, waiting to hear the familiar sounds of their garage door opening, the key turning in the lock and feet climbing the stairs. Michael had called Ellen from work yesterday afternoon to say that he'd been roped into having dinner with clients and would be late.

"That's fine." Her voice had sounded pinched. "I never count on you being here for dinner, anyway."

Ellen glanced at the clock above the stove. It was now 7:05 a.m. and Michael was still not home. She walked through the kitchen and into the front hallway. "Lucy, Eric, it's time for breakfast!" she called up the stairs, her voice a sad song. Since dinner was so often impossible with Michael's job and with Lucy and Eric's various commitments to their clubs and athletic teams, Ellen tried to make sure her family at least ate breakfast together.

"Mom," Lucy called back, sounding surprised. "Eric had swimming this morning, remember? He's already gone." Ellen had forgotten. She must have nodded off again and missed her son's soft morning sounds: water from the faucet, a bagel popping up from the toaster, and the squeaking of his chair against the kitchen floor. Living only a block away from Thomas Jefferson Junior High School meant that Ellen was freed from much of the car pool duties other mothers complained about. But sometimes, she wished she *did* have those car rides. Then she'd have a chance to really talk to her children and help them work through any of the problems she knew they must encounter daily at school and on the weekends with their friends. *I used to be a teenager, too*, she always told them, wanting Lucy and Eric to feel comfortable asking her advice.

"And I have to go in early to make up the algebra test I missed last week," Lucy reminded her. "I'll just grab a banana or something."

"Oh, right, I remember." Ellen's voice faltered. She could imagine Lucy upstairs now, her face only inches from the mirror as she carefully applied peach lip gloss, glittery-green eye shadow and waterproof mascara. Ellen thought fourteen was much too young for makeup, but Michael let her daughter get away with just about anything, and it was no longer worth Ellen's energy to argue with Lucy about it every morning.

Ellen walked back into the kitchen and turned off the oven. She used her oven mitts to carefully remove the egg casserole, planning to reheat it the next morning. Then, she put away two of the sky blue plates, two of the flatware sets, and two of the glasses. Minutes later, Lucy scurried down the stairs and flew through the kitchen, running late as usual. She pulled her winter coat from the closet and was out the door before even putting it on. As almost an afterthought, she called out behind her: "Bye mom! I'll see you this afternoon!"

Michael hadn't been lying to his wife about having a dinner meeting. Last night had begun over appetizers in a dimly lit Italian restaurant with kindly waiters in white coats who brought glass after glass of red zinfandel to him.

Michael's dinner companions consisted of his partner, Ed Yordy, along with Bob Wilson and Ruth Rimmer, the president and lead in-house counsel of Arametrics, the largest pharmaceutical distributor in the region. Ed was in rare form, having the waiter pour glasses of this and that for his guests while sucking up to Bob and Ruth both through his words and reverent tone.

"So Arametrics' first office was in your attic," Ed said, his teeth gleaming. Michael wondered if he had them professionally whitened. "I heard you stayed up working all night sometimes, until you had to leave for your eight-to-five job that paid the bills. Incredible."

"Sometimes I can't believe it either, Ed. We started small, but before we knew it, things were heating up and business was growing like wild flowers," said Bob, who droned on and on about how he'd initially gotten business from some smaller pharmacies that had decided to stick with Arametrics as they continued to grow. He liked comparing Arametrics to all sorts of foliage: "One of those big firms

136

offered to buy me out, but I wanted to stay with it, establish some roots," and "If you treat customers honestly, they'll grow like ivy on a fence," and "I knew when I got Ruth on board everything would run as smooth as daisies."

As smooth as daisies? Michael thought. He took another gulp of wine.

Ed only nodded intently, occasionally flashing those professionally polished teeth. Ruth also smiled, but it seemed forced. She had stopped drinking and ran her fingers absently through her thick brown hair. She checked her watch and straightened her jacket. She coughed. It was 8:42 p.m. and Ruth looked ready to call it a night.

"Well, this has been some evening," Michael suddenly interrupted, cutting off Bob in the middle of some leafy comment. Ed and Bob turned toward him, shocked. Michael wanted to say something clever, something to impress Ruth and pull her back into the conversation. Instead, he said, "And I must say, the thought of being able to work with you two long-term is quite a rosy idea." Michael was a little drunk and he giggled at his own joke.

Ed's head was tilted and he looked at Michael quizzically, as if trying to figure out some puzzle behind his words.

"What I mean," Michael said, jerking his left arm off the table for emphasis, "is that . . ." and then in slow motion, the back of his hand made contact with his glass of red wine. The glass lifted up off the table, flying across toward Bob. Ruth, sitting on Michael's left, did a sort of dive over the table and caught the glass in mid air before even a drop escaped. Ed's mouth was open in a horrified triangle; Bob's eyes were wide as cucumber slices. Ruth teetered for a moment, trying to regain balance, and then successfully set the glass back down next to Michael. She smoothed out her skirt and sat back down in her chair, the trace of a triumphant smile on her face.

For a second, no one spoke, and then Bob, realizing he once again had a captive audience, continued, "Like I was saying, she's as smooth as daisies . . ."

Ruth had gone to undergrad at the University of Colorado and then Washington University Law School. She enjoyed finding solutions to complex problems, anywhere from the *New York Times* crossword puzzle to the hidden inconsistencies in a contract. She was smart and well respected, but had few real friends (the kind that just called to chat on a rainy afternoon) and felt more comfortable by herself than with other people. She was glad when the dinner was finally over, when she picked up her jacket from the coat check and wished everyone a good evening. Her smile, then, was genuine.

Ed was nervous and kept trying to throw out last-attempt compliments, shaking both of their hands with sweaty fingers as the valet drove up in his black BMW.

Let us sell you the new computer hardware you need, his eyes silently begged. *Let us network your company's computers into one cohesive unit! Please, let us fulfill every last one of your technological fantasies!* Out loud, he said, "I look forward to working with you. It's been a pleasure, a *pleasure*, spending the evening with you." Ed nodded his head up-and-down for emphasis.

"A pleasure," Michael echoed, who stood slightly behind them.

"Excuse me sir, your car is waiting," the valet interrupted them, pointing to Ed's car.

"Thank you," Ed said, and then spent an awkward moment searching through his pockets before handing the valet a bundle of bills and saying, "That's for all of us." Ed was still nodding up-and-down as he slid into the front seat.

"Well, thank you Ed," said Bob. "I appreciate you taking us out."

"Yes, thank you," Ruth said, smiling sweetly, hoping to still be able to catch the late news on Channel 5. "It was a delightful evening."

"We'll talk soon," Ed called out to them, the valet closing the door behind him.

Bob's car was next in line. Ruth rubbed her hands together, cupped them over her mouth and blew into them for warmth.

Bob wished Ruth a pleasant evening, hopped into his car, and drove away, without as much as a backward glance in Michael's direction.

"I actually didn't valet," Michael said to Ruth. "Did you?"

"Yes, I'm sure it will be right here. Go ahead, I'll be fine," she said, her eyes scanning the parking lot for her navy Jetta.

"I probably shouldn't be driving yet anyway," he told her.

Ruth tried to hide her annoyance. "Whatever you want to do.

But don't worry about me. Really, I'm fine."

Michael didn't move; her car was still nowhere in sight. Finally, a boy in a faded orange jacket walked up to Ruth, his shoulders up in a delayed shrug and said, "Ma'am, I apologize, but your car won't start."

Michael Cohen had met Ellen Wise three years ago on the shoulder of Highway 40 heading east towards St. Louis. She was leaning over the open hood of her car, shivering, wearing only a black cocktail dress with a red shawl. Snow glistened in her hair. Even though he had been driving for over seventeen hours straight, something about her tiny frame hovering over a smoking car convinced him to pull over.

He rolled down his window and called out to her, "Do you need some help, ma'am?" Ellen told him later that the way he said it reminded her of a television commercial.

She'd looked over at him with tears frozen onto her face. "No, I'm fine," she stammered, teeth chattering.

"Look, you're going to freeze out there. Literally," Michael insisted. "Let me at least drive you to a pay phone so you can call somebody to help you."

She stood completely still for a moment, considering her options, (freezing to death versus a tall, dark—and possibly dangerous—stranger) and then closed the car's hood and wobbled over to his truck through the snow. She was shaking almost uncontrollably by then. Michael wrapped his jacket around her, keeping his arm close to her body longer than necessary. He pulled back out onto the highway carefully; the snow was coming down hard. "Where should I take you?" he asked. "Do you live near?"

"About fifteen minutes. Just stay on the highway for now," she suggested. "You?"

"Oh, about seventeen hours," he said casually, giving her a sideways glance, grinning.

She still had the jacket pulled tight around her. "Are you on a trip?"

"I guess you could say that." He paused for a moment. "Where were you going tonight, all dressed with no coat?"

"Not too smart, huh?" She gave a quick laugh. "I was coming

139

home from a Christmas party."

"Coming home? It's only a little after eight!"

"It started snowing pretty hard and, well," her voice trailed off. "It's the first one I've gone to alone, without my husband, and it just felt like it was time to go."

"I'm so sorry," Michael responded.

"Oh, no," she laughed again, nervously this time. "Don't be sorry. He's fine, just not with me, anymore."

Ellen suggested a nearby diner, the kind with swivel chairs at the counter, where she called a tow truck and discovered that, due to the weather, she was pretty far down the list for a tow. She and Michael ordered two cups of coffee and two jelly doughnuts and passed the time by talking and laughing about all the things people do when they first meet and want to know each other better. In less than ninety minutes, Ellen was convinced that Michael's ex-boss in Seattle was an insensitive ass ("He told me that unless my work made a monumental improvement, he was going to have to cut my salary by a third. But I was already working over sixty hours a week! How could I do more than that?"), that his ex-wife had been miserably unsupportive ("Sweetheart," she'd said, "sixty hours a week doesn't mean a thing if you're doing shoddy work."), and that Michael was exceedingly courageous to just pack up everything he owned and move across the country to start over. In less than ninety minutes, Michael was convinced that St. Louis was as good a place as any to start over.

After they met the tow truck and Ellen explained to the red-bearded driver where to drop off her temperamental car, Michael drove Ellen home. He was quiet, and she patiently directed him to the left, and then right, and then left again. Ten minutes later, they were parked in front of her house.

"Are you going to be okay?" Michael asked.

"I think so," she said. "Thanks for the ride. I probably *would* have frozen to death out there. I guess it's time to give in and buy a cell phone." She began to take off his coat.

"No," he said, "keep it for tonight. You shouldn't be walking outside without a coat."

"But you don't live around here!" she protested.

"Oh, I don't think I better be driving much farther tonight anyway. Why don't I come over and pick it up tomorrow? That way I can make sure everything is okay with your car, too."

She smiled. "Okay."

Tonight, with Ruth, reminded Michael a little of that night, except, of course, that Ruth was much less interested in his help. "Thank you for waiting with me," she said, "but really, I called my friend and he should be here any time to pick me up." Unlike Ellen, she had a cell phone.

Ruth hated situations like this: a man feeling like he had to wait around to protect a woman even when there was really nothing the man could do to help.

"No way," Michael said, "I've already made a big enough idiot out of myself tonight. I'm not just going to leave you here, stranded."

"I'll be fine. I'll wait inside."

"If you don't mind, I'll just wait with you. I want to make sure you're okay."

Ruth bit down hard on her bottom lip to keep from saying anything else. They sat at the bar together on tall wooden chairs. She ordered a tonic with lime; he ordered another glass of wine. "So what do you do for fun?" Michael asked.

"What do *you* do?" Ruth shot back.

"Let's see." He drummed his fingers against his chin for a moment, thinking. "I enjoy movies, watching my kid's swim meets and having a drink with a beautiful woman."

"Are you flirting with me?" Ruth gave him a sideways glance. "Because if you are, I'd ask you to please stop." Ruth felt uncomfortable with this kind of I'd-like-to-get-to-know-you-better attention.

Michael sighed, resigned. "Okay, I only enjoy movies and swim meets. What do you like?"

"I teach painting to kids on Wednesdays." She played with the silver bracelet on her left wrist, twirling it around. "All different kinds, from watercolors to finger painting. I enjoy that," she said, sounding almost surprised at her answer.

"Really? My son takes lessons at the old art museum."

"That's where I teach!" She sounded excited now. "What's his name?"

"Eric. Eric Wise."

"Yes, yes, I know Eric. He's wonderful. Very talented," she said, looking at Michael carefully. "But Eric," she continued slowly, "Eric said his father passed away a few years ago."

"Really?" Michael stopped to think. "Well, that doesn't make any sense. I'm Eric's stepfather, actually. But his father, his real father, is still alive. He moved to L.A. a few years ago and, even though I guess he doesn't see Eric and Lucy as much as he should, he does as much as he can for them, considering the distance." He met Ruth's eyes. "Dead, huh?"

"Dead," she nodded. "Well, Eric creates these fabulous paintings, but they're very dark. Just last week he used violet and black to paint the background of a so-called Christmas scene full of grayish monsters decorating a pine tree with old shoes and socks. Have you seen it?"

"Of course," Michael lied.

"So what do you think it means?"

"I don't know." Michael barely had time to acknowledge Eric's painting, much less examine it for some inner meaning.

"He said his father was murdered, actually."

"He's told you quite a bit, it seems," Michael said, his drink making his voice sound much more concerned than he usually felt. "I wish he could talk to *me*." And, for just a moment, Michael wished they *could* be like a regular father and son, pals, who threw around the football on crisp autumn mornings.

Although Michael genuinely did think Eric was a good kid, he also knew that Eric was too protective of his mother (always reminding him how upset Ellen was when he was even a *minute* late) and too loyal to his father ("Dad told me he might not be able to call tonight because he's working overtime to help pay for my plane ticket next summer.") to ever carelessly toss around a football with him. And, in reality, Michael considered this a blessing. He was nervous around teenagers, unsure what to say and how to act. It was enough for Michael to watch from the stands, feeling proud that he provided Eric with the necessary food, clothing and shelter to live a comfortable life.

"I believe painting comes from deep inside, and I talk to my students about this. It comes with the territory."

"I see."

Ruth saw the hurt in Michael's expression. She placed her hand over his, seeing him not as a salesman, but as a father, with a little boy to worry about.

Eric was, at that very moment, in his room with the door shut. His television was turned up loud enough to block out sounds from the rest of the house, like his mother's incessant crying, but he wasn't watching it. Instead, he was stretched out on his bed, staring up the ceiling, hating.

He hated so much that it actually scared him.

Michael had started staying out late about once a month. On those nights, Eric's mother stayed awake downstairs until early in the morning, polishing the silver, washing the crystal or dusting the bookshelves. Eventually, she'd make her way up the stairs, into her room, where she hiccupped down tears until, finally, Michael would pull into the driveway only a few hours before he was expected at work. Eric had seen this all before. He knew that once a month would soon turn into once a week, and this time the hate pressed against his chest like a balloon that could explode at any time. In fact, he had even called his dad last night and begged to come live with him.

"With me? In L.A.? Aw, Eric, L.A. isn't any place for a kid to grow up. You know that."

"Then come back home, please. Get a place back here." He was on the brink of tears, trying desperately to hold them back.

"There's no place for me there anymore, kiddo, you know that," his dad said. "Maybe this summer we can work something out with your mom, and you can stay out here for a few weeks."

His sister banged on the wall, "Turn that down! I'm trying to sleep!"

"You are not," he called back. "You're trying to talk on the phone."

"Mom!" Lucy called for backup. "Mom!"

Eric reached for the remote and turned the sound up a level. He could almost see his mother at the window, the way she looked when he sat on the stairs, peeked around the corner and secretly watched her during those early morning hours: her forehead pressed against the glass, waiting for headlights that would never come.

Ruth called her friend to explain that she had found another ride home, and she drove Michael's Audi TT to her house.

"Maybe you should stay here tonight," she told Michael. "I don't think you're in any condition to drive home."

"Maybe," he said. His head was spinning.

"You can call your wife and sleep on the couch."

A laugh escaped between his parted lips. "Of course. Of course."

He punched the numbers into the phone carefully. *Beep-beep-beep-beep.* "It's busy," he told Ruth.

"I laid a blanket and pillow on the couch for you."

Michael still held the phone in his hand. Ruth had taken off her shoes and her pantyhose. Her hair was pulled back into a ponytail, and she looked much younger somehow. He hung up the phone carefully and walked over to her, placing his right hand on her right hip.

"Michael," she warned, without moving.

He leaned towards her and with his lips only a centimeter from hers, he reached around to unzip her dress.

The first time Michael hadn't come home, Ellen had called all of the hospitals, all of their friends, even the police. The next morning, Michael had phoned her from work, as though everything was normal, explaining that he just drank a little too much and spent the night on a friend's couch.

"What friend? What friend!" Ellen had shrieked. "I called all of your friends!"

"Joe, from the office," Michael had calmly explained, repeating lines he'd heard in movies. "I'm sorry Ellen, I *should* have called. I *meant* to call."

One night had turned into dozens. Ellen should have known from the beginning, but she was still so heartbroken from Brian leaving, and she'd felt a sense of victory when she found Michael to show off to everyone who felt sorry for her and secretly thought that

144

she should forgive Brian and take him back because she would never be able to do any better anyway. Michael was handsome—no, handsome wasn't the right word. He was beautiful, with thick black hair, quiet eyes, and long eyelashes that, in reality, only a woman deserved. His skin fit tightly around his body, and he looked at her, right in the eyes, when she talked. It had seemed like fate when she found him on the side of the road that night. "Stay," she had told him. "Stay."

And when Brian called and begged her to forgive him and to think about the kids she could say: "It's over. I've found someone else." And at the time, that had been enough.

When Michael woke up, two-and-a-half hours later, and saw the bright red numbers call out 3:03 a.m., he wondered where he was. When he flipped over and saw Ruth there, breathing softly through parted lips, images of last night flashed through his mind. *Ellen*. Had he called her? He remembered holding the phone and dialing the number, but had he talked to her?

He pulled himself out of the bed's unfamiliar softness. His head throbbed and his left arm was numb. Michael found his pants and socks in the living room, his shirt and undershirt in the hall, wrapped together in a ball, and his boxers next to the bed. His keys were on the kitchen table. Michael took a glass from the cabinet above the microwave, filled it with tap water, gulped it down and set it in the sink. He unlocked the front door, slipped out and closed the door behind him with a quiet clink.

Driving home on an almost empty highway, Michael began to construct his story.

Michael spent most days feeling guilty, knowing that this type of behavior was exactly why Ellen had left her first husband. Ellen was such a kind woman; she deserved better. She had showered him with affection when he was unemployed, broke and very alone. Back then it hadn't seemed so bad to have someone gently pushing him. (*Maybe you should think about going back to school. An M.B.A. maybe? And, I'll talk to Gregg Greeler. Oh I can't wait for you to meet Gregg; he was president and I was vice president of our high school class. Oh yes, Gregg's such a sweetheart, and he's always looking for someone with sales experience.*) The problem was that, only three years after they married, Michael could barely breathe in that house. Every moment was scheduled. It was like one of those Boy Scout camps.

Breakfast started promptly at 7:00. (*Honey, do you remember Debra Mae, from church? Well, Debra Mae made the most delicious egg casserole for that fundraiser last weekend. She is such a sweet woman and was so pleased when I asked her for the recipe. I can't wait for you to try it!*). And he mustn't forget, Eric had a swim meet at 4:00. (*Why don't I pick you up from work so we can drive together? That way maybe we can all catch a bite afterwards. Have you been to that new neighborhood grill on Watson? It has such a variety. Nutritious and delicious!*) The Carters were coming over for trivia at 7:30. (*You remember Kelly and George don't you? I volunteer with Kelly at the hospital? She's a doll. You'll love her, dear. And George, he's such a peach.*) Saturday, the washing machine started whirling at 6:45 a.m. The vacuum was running by 7:15 and at 7:45, he was expected to be in the yard. (*Why, I hope George and Kelly didn't think our lawn was completely overrun with weeds last night. I'll be out in a jiffy to help!*)

Ellen had drifted off the first time at about 3:45 a.m. and so didn't hear the car pull into the driveway. Perhaps she would have woken up if Michael had opened the garage or unlocked the front door, but instead he left the car on the street and walked around the house to the back door, which opened up into the downstairs family room. His heart was pounding; blood slammed against the insides of his head and there was a squeezing against the center his chest. His hands shook as he lifted up the mat to find the little silver key that opened the sliding door. He pushed the door open with a quiet whisssh.

The television was on, but the sound was off. A mop of blond shaggy hair poked up from over the back of the couch. Two angry blue eyes on the face of a thirteen year old met his two tired brown ones.

"Eric, buddy," Michael called out. "What are you doing up?"

Eric clicked off the television and turned to face him.

"What are you doing out?" Eric slung back.

"I was with a client," he said, barely able to get the words out. He was sweating now, a drop falling off the edge of his nose. The pain from his chest spread through his shoulders and neck and then

146

raced down through his arms.

"What's wrong with you?" Eric asked. "Don't think I'm going to feel sorry for you!"

"Son, call 911."

"Oh, come on." Eric tried to keep his voice down, so as not to wake his mother. He watched Michael's eyes dart furiously around the room, searching for the cordless phone. When Michael spotted it on top of the couch, next to Eric, he staggered over to it, hand outreached.

"No!" Eric grabbed the phone first, then jumped up and over to the still open sliding door. He threw the receiver as far as he could into the back yard. "No!"

"Jesus Christ, Eric! I think I'm having a goddamn heart attack," his voice sputtered as he pushed the boy away and staggered into the back yard. Eric raced over to the cradle and unplugged it, watching Michael fumble through the wet grass searching for the useless piece of plastic, his head spinning, feeling dizzy like on one of those rides at the school carnival that whip you around in endless circles. Snow had just started falling.

The phone rang at about 9:30 that morning. Ellen was downstairs, hunting around for Michael's address book, and couldn't find the cordless phone. She took the steps two at a time upstairs and answered with a shaky, "Hello?"

"Ellen?" The voice boomed.

"Yes?"

"Ed Yordy here. How you doing?"

"Okay, I guess."

"I'm looking for Michael. Is he around?"

"No, I'm sorry."

"Well, do you know where he's at by any chance?"

"Work, I guess," Ellen said faintly.

"No, he's not here yet. Maybe just running late, huh?"

"Maybe. I didn't see him this morning."

"Well, if he happens to call you before I reach him, tell him I need to talk to him right away. We had a meeting scheduled for first thing this morning."

"Sure." Ellen said. Then suddenly, she remembered the voices she had heard last night while dozing on the couch: her son's voice yelling, the door sliding shut with a slam. At the time, she had tried to block them out, pulling the thin cotton blanket over her head.

She dropped the phone, hearing the receiver call out to her, "Ellen? Ellen?" She ran down the stairs, over to the glass door and saw in the middle of the back yard her husband lying there under a thin layer of snow, with the phone inches from his hand.

Eric had sat on the couch until 5:45 a.m., terrified. He'd left for swim practice at 6:15 and was in the pool by 6:45. He swam down to the bottom of the blue water, holding his breath until he thought his lungs would burst, and then even a little longer. He crashed up to the surface, sputtering for air, wanting to understand for himself what Michael had felt only a few hours ago.

"Eric," his coach called. "You okay over there?"

"Fine!" he called back. "I'm just fine." Then he flipped over onto his back and floated for a moment, breathing heavy. His pupils were large as he stared up into the fluorescent lights, which reflected down onto a boy who, later, would never be able to forgive his mother for forgiving him.

Our judges were surprised—very pleasantly—to learn that you, a well-known poet and editor, are also a talented fiction writer. "Freezer" was their unanimous choice for first prize in this contest. Could you give us some background about you as a fiction writer? (With whom did you study? How long have you been writing? What, if anything, caused the emphasis on poetry?)

I began as a fiction writer. When I was a college student, it seemed like a romantic thing to be. I spent a lot of time hunched over a computer with a cigarette and a glass of wine, typing away, imagining I was Ernest Hemingway or Saul Bellow. I cultivated what I thought was a writerly persona and wore eccentric, polyester clothes, then enrolled in a couple workshops, first with Phyllis Rose and then with James Finney Boylan, and took copious notes.

When I graduated from Wesleyan, I took a job with the NewsHour with Jim Lehrer, spent the day researching stories for the senior reporters and the evenings working on fiction which I then dutifully sent off to quarterlies, sometimes with success. After a year of living in poverty in a sewing closet in SE Washington, D.C., I realized that my interest in fiction surpassed my interest in politics, so I took a scholarship offer from the Hollins Writing Program to work on my writing full time in the Blue Ridge Mountains. I intended even then to be a fiction writer, though I'd been writing and publishing poems as well. It was at Hollins, where the faculty required students to work in both genres, that I became attracted to the lyric intensity and economy of poetry. At that time, I largely gave up on fiction.

Do you consider yourself a Missouri writer simply because you have lived here for a long time or is there something about the Missouri experience that has transformed you, is reflected in both your fiction and your poetry?

Scary question! I've moved around so much in my life—I grew

up in Cleveland, went to boarding school, then to college in Connecticut. I've also lived in Germany, Washington, D.C., Virginia, Nebraska, St. Louis... The funny thing is, though, that after seven years in small-town Missouri, I still don't think of myself as a Missouri writer. In fact, I'm not sure what region I belong to. My newest work is mostly about ancient Rome and when I think about what inspires me most geographically, it's my fantasies about great, complex ancient cities.

Do you consider yourself a fiction writer now? What projects do you currently have underway? Or plan for the future?

I'd love to write fiction again, but I haven't spent as much time on it as I should. I have a book of poems I'm cleaning up right now which should be published in 2005. It's called *Fallen From a Chariot* and is largely about political and personal disasters—the fall of the Empire (which I can't help thinking of as both our own and the one centered in ancient Rome), airplane crashes, auto wrecks. I'm also editing a new book devoted to great, never anthologized, overlooked poems.

What about this story in particular? How did it come about?

When I was living in Washington, I had a very wealthy friend. His family owned a number of television stations, a large bank, houses all over the country and in Europe. I wondered what it would be like to come from such a family—to receive as a graduation gift a new house in the toniest part of the city. He was a very kind young man, but I was jealous of him. His parents had a beautiful mansion which became the setting for "Freezer." They even had an enormous, sinister, coffin-like freezer in the garage. When I looked at it, I remembered stories my parents told me about little kids who died playing around freezers which, when closed, were impossible to open from the inside.

152

"Freezer" is light horror, rather tongue-in-cheek, and highly literary, particularly in language and symbolism. What were you conscious of attempting? (at the simplest? at the most complex?)

Yes, I was conscious of the symbolism and goals of the story even as I giggled as I wrote it. I was broke when I wrote the first draft, living in a windowless, basement apartment with a roommate I didn't particularly like. All around me—this was in Arlington, Virginia—I saw poverty and crime, felt the dangerous neighborhoods creeping up on my own. I thought about my wealthy friend and imagined—this may sound sort of immature—that with that kind of wealth must come a certain amorality.

As I cleaned up the story through several drafts over quite a few years—I kept putting the story away and coming back to it—it turned into a little parable about the impermanence of good fortune, about glacial shifts in class and neighborhood. I think it took a few years for the "message" of the story to crystallize.

At one point, I showed it to a friend who told me she'd seen almost the same plot—a woman murders a man and hides him in a freezer—on TV. I put the story away then, discouraged, though in retrospect I suppose this plot has been done more than just a couple times. An enormous freezer would be such a good place to preserve a body, after all. And I'm glad that friend inspired me to put "Freezer" away for a few years, because I think the newer draft—a draft that came with some distance—is better than the original.

Did you have a particular audience in mind, i.e. literary as opposed to general?

When I write, I'm the audience. If I think too much about others—editors, friends, readers—I get blocked.

How would you distinguish the literary story (if, that is, you make that distinction)?

Nope. I don't like that distinction. When I come to a story, I ask myself a couple questions. First, what is the goal of the story?

153

Does it seem worthwhile? Is it merely prurient or morbid? Does it evolve after more than one reading? Is the goal worthwhile and ambitious? After that, how does it achieve its goal? I admire it if it seems ambitious, worthwhile, and successful. Of course, I enjoy stories that are merely exciting... I'm just not sure I admire them all that much.

Are you a reader of genre fiction, e.g. mysteries, horror, fantasy? Whom do you consider masters of craft? And why?

Yes. I love genre fiction. Mysteries, science fiction, horror—I'll read them all. I'm often frustrated because it's hard to find good examples. Perhaps this is because I don't have a ready community of readers of genre fiction around who can suggest titles, so I go at it fairly randomly. Philip K. Dick, Michael Connelly, H. P. Lovecraft, Henry James, Stephen Saylor—they've written some of my favorite genre stories. The masters? James, Dick, Lovecraft, Poe, Highsmith, Hawthorne. There are so many.

What will make you stop reading a book after only a few pages? Or do you go to the end, however bitter the journey?

I have a rule which my girlfriend thinks is compulsive and silly. If I get to page 50 in a book, I always complete it. I'm free to quit, though, during the first 50 pages. I think I'm stopped by the same things that stop most readers (and writers)—clichés, clunky prose, poorly drawn characters, familiar plots. I recently picked up a horror novel called Incubus because the dust jacket said it was a "New York Times Notable Book of the Year." I made it to page 50, at which point the book became immediately awful. I slogged through the rest of it, though, because of my rule. I hated every page.

You are at least semi-expert in Greek and Roman history and archaeology—among, I might add, other areas—and that specialized knowledge is intricately woven throughout your work. Was this interest in your early writing? Did you deliberately develop it?

My interest in classical history came to me all of a sudden one day and has never let up. About six years ago, I visited Bath, England, and took a guided tour of the ruins of the ancient Roman baths. I didn't know anything about ancient Rome then. In fact, I probably couldn't have told you precisely when the Roman Empire existed, except to say that it was a couple thousand years ago. The baths were amazing to me, though—the complex plumbing, the heating system, the intricacy of the structure. On the wall were displayed hundreds of curse tablets—note card-sized squares of lead on which the ancients had written curses which they tossed into the baths the same way we toss pennies in fountains hoping our wishes will be granted. One man wished for the death of another who had stolen his goats. A woman wanted her betraying lover killed. A third desired money to pay for a trip to visit his family. The tablets were so personal and human that I spent hours reading them, then went back the next day to read them all again. I spent a couple hours sitting on the edge of the main bath trying to recreate the structure in my head, to fill it with the people who'd written the curse tablets. I'd never thought about history in such personal, visceral terms before. I suppose that that was the single most important day so far in my writing life. It's inspired an enormous amount of research, a great deal of thought, a new book, and the beginnings of yet another.

Does such an interest come to fruition, fulfillment and end, replaced with something else?

I hope it doesn't ever end. The Roman Empire is too complex, vast, and important for it ever to come to fulfillment. If it does, it will because I have failed the subject.

In a classroom visit, Richard Yates once remarked that he could never get a particular story ending right, and let the story be published though he was dissatisfied with the ending. Do you ever let a piece appear in print before you're satisfied? Have you ever rewritten one after it was published?

When I finish writing a poem or story, I'm usually convinced it's the greatest work of literature ever written by anybody at any time. The next morning, though, I see its flaws and, most of the time, tuck it away on my hard drive. I try not to send anything out that I don't think is complete, though I've certainly changed my mind about work after it's been published. And I've rewritten work for book publication after it appeared in a magazine.

Have you ever destroyed a work and sorely wanted it back? When? What was it?

Yes, by accident. When I was living in Nebraska, I wrote a story about a young man driving home one night from his sister's funeral. He sees a barn burning just off the road and pulls over to watch. After a few minutes, a horse staggers through the burning doors. It's on fire, too, and walks a few steps into the field, flames rising from its back, then falls over and dies. Just as I was completing a revision of that story, my computer died. I've never written it again.

What is your writing process? It must be highly efficient, given that at the age of 33, you have published two anthologies, two collections, become Director of Creative Writing at a Missouri University, and editor of a major literary publication. How do you do it?

There aren't many distractions in my little town, so I spend a lot of time writing. I only write at night, usually with music playing. If I haven't written in a while, I grow cranky and irritable. I revise a great deal. I read my work out loud and, if I'm writing poetry, I read it backwards, judging every line in isolation. I scan my work, count syllables, fuss with lineation. I'm not sure there's much else to it.

What crossover, if any, do you see between fiction writing of any kind and poetry?

My own poems are very narrative, though I rarely imagine the narrative voice to be my own. Right now, I'm writing poems that (at

156

least attempt to) take place in three times simultaneously. They have as their focus not a single narrative line, but a particular place—generally, a place in Rome—and shift between the present, the distant past, and an imagined future. I'm trying to write poems in which those three narrative lines connect, in which Nero can watch Rome burn while, thousands of years in the future, bombs fall on the ruins of his palace and, fifty years after that, a young man sits on a park bench in the same place reading a book. The project is challenging, but ultimately relies on many of the same tools I use when I write fiction—setting, character development, plot. Poetry, though, is very freeing for me; I feel less weighed down by the expectations of the genre and, thus, able to try crazy things.

Traditionally, genre writing is not allowed in required creative writing coursework, but genres may be the focus of special classes. What's your stand on this restriction?

I don't like that restriction, but suspect I'm almost alone in my belief. Genre writing presents students with challenges in addition to those that come with traditional fiction. For instance, if a student is writing fantasy, she's expected not only to come up with viable characters, a good story, tensions, dialogue, etc., but must also invent a convincing, interesting, original new world for her readers—and she must do it gracefully. In a way, the additional expectations make genre writing more challenging for beginning students, though many of the elements of a successful genre story are the same as they would be for a more traditional work of fiction. I don't encourage my students to write genre fiction, but I don't prohibit it, either.

According to a recent article in the NY Times, there's almost a direct line between creative writing courses and Hollywood productions—first novels becoming movies, students writing for movies. As Director of Creative Writing at Central, do you find the Hollywood market a specific goal of your writing students?

Yes, I think that whether they know it or not, many of my

students are writing for Hollywood. So many of their stories are obviously inspired by what I see as the worst in Hollywood movies—wooden characters, mindless violence, cliché-ridden plots, familiar dialogue. Rarely does a student come to me wanting to write a Hollywood movie, though—and, generally, the influence of Hollywood is destructive to their own stories.

Did you consider using a pseudonym? Why didn't you? What do you see as the pros and cons of using one?

I've thought about it. Prufer is such a clunky name. It sounds too much like T.S. Eliot's "Prufrock," and calls up images of an inhibited, stunted man. I'd love to be named Bronco Savagewood or Violet Windspeare, but at this point it's too late to change my name.

What was your best publication experience, something that surprised you, perhaps, or was just rewarding?

I've been lucky with publishing. The first piece I ever sent off was accepted and, though I've had many rejections, most of my better work has found sympathetic editors. Last week, I had a long poem win a Pushcart Prize. The editors of the magazine that first published it sent a bouquet of flowers. To be honest, I was so touched I almost cried. I don't think I've ever been sent flowers by anyone but my sister. And I've received letters from readers, which is very rewarding. Sometimes, I suspect no one reads my work—that I write it, it gets published, then just disappears—so when I get a letter from a reader I'm overjoyed.

And the worst experience?

Typos. I spend so much time fussing with my work, both as a writer and editor. I can't stand to see them.

You have an admirable history of supporting other writers by discovering and publishing new poets and fiction writers, but also by submitting your own excellent work to emerging and small presses. Many successful writers submit their work only to top markets. What philosophy allows you to be generous with your work in that way?

I think this is less a philosophy than a strong belief. I believe that most of the best writing in America is being published by small, independent, and university presses. Since they rely less on the whims of the market, editors at small presses are free to experiment, to sponsor writers who are good, regardless of how marketable their work is. This is very freeing for the editor and, of course, wonderful for the reader who has the drive to seek out small press publications. That's why I write for the small press and it's also why I work as a small-press editor. There's a great deal of freedom on both sides.

What advice do you have for writers entering contests?

Oh, be very, very careful. There are so many scams. Check out the contest before you submit. And don't be discouraged when you don't win. Every time I send work to a contest—which I rarely do these days—I consider my reading fee a donation to the press, then try to forget that I sent my work at all. That way, when I get a form rejection, I'm not discouraged.

And what would you advise writers about submitting work to small presses?

I always used to hear that editors of small presses really love reading submissions, discovering new writers, promoting them. I never believed it. But now that I edit a small press—both a journal and a book series—I know it's true. Small press editors really do love the moment when they discover something fine. Of course, they're overwhelmed with manuscripts and make frequent mistakes. I've turned down quite a few pieces that, in retrospect, I wish I'd published. My advice: don't take rejection seriously, and don't be

159

angry when editors turn you down. Simultaneously submit, if you can. Find an editor who seems to like your work and stick with her.

Notes on Contributors

Perry Beam (Mayview) was born and reared in Missouri. He received a Bachelor of Arts in English at Central Missouri State University. Until marrying in 1990, he made his living by playing piano and still performs regularly. He teaches English at Yung-Da college of Engineering and Technology, Ping-Tung, Taiwan. With his wife and two sons, he resides in Taiwan most of the year, returning to spend summers on their farm in Lafayette County.

Catherine Berry (St. Louis) supports her writing by working as a textile artist.

Matt Bird-Meyer (Warrensburg) is editor-in-chief and co-founder of the *Warrensburg Free Press* and works simultaneously as news editor of the *Lee's Summit Journal*. He is the founder of the Dragonfly Extravaganza in Warrensburg, hosting a collection of local and regional talent, including visual arts, music and spoken word during these gatherings. He attended Northeast Missouri State University (now Truman State University) for two years, studying creative writing and visual art. He graduated from Central Missouri State University in 1997 with a Bachelor of Science in Journalism. During his time as a student reporter with Cental's *Muleskinner*, he served as assistant news editor. He writes poetry and short fiction.

Jo Gallagher (St. Louis), a nurse by education, owns and operates the oldest costume shop in the nation. Relatively new to writing poetry and fiction, she has had several articles published in *The Costumer* and *Art Hazard News*, trade publications, and has published two industry-related, humorous poems in *The Costumer*. She was a finalist in the poetry competition at the Heartland Writers Guild (HWG) conference in June of 2002. Her short fiction has won two on-line competitions and placed in others. She is a member of the HWG and of Works in Progress, a local writers' forum.

Tim Hammack (St. Charles) served for four years as a Korean linguist with the Army. After military service, he attended the University of Illinois at Urbana-Champaign, and graduated with a

Bachelor of Science in Computer Science. He states that he has "traveled across India, China, and Japan with little more than a *Lonely Planet's Guidebook*, a smattering of local languages, and a sturdy roll of toilet paper."

Donn Irving (Centerview) is the pen name of Donn Irving Blevins. He received a doctorate in veterinary medicine from the University of Missouri and a Master of Arts in Literature from Southwest Missouri State/Baker University. His fiction has won numerous awards, including second place (and publication), Woodley Press Robert Gross Award for a novella; first place, Kansas Voices Contest; finalist Nelson Algren Contest; finalist Faulkner/Pirate's Alley contest; finalist and runner-up, Raymond Carver contests; Hugh Luke Award by *Negative Capability*; and a Pushcart nomination. His short stories have appeared in *American Literary Review*, *New Letters*, *The Crescent Review*, *The Natural Bridge*, *The Cream City Review*, *The Chariton Review*, *Negative Capability*, *Reed Magazine*, *Pleiades*, *Farmer's Market*, *Habersham Review*, and other places.

Emily Spreng Lowery (St. Louis) graduated with a Bachelor of Arts in English Writing from Millikin University in Decatur, Illinois. She is currently enrolled in the MFA program at the University of Missouri –St. Louis where she is a fiction editor with the literary journal *Natural Bridge*.

Judith Kelvin Miller (Clayton) is a writer and photographer. She has published over 15 papers in peer-reviewed science journals, has an essay forthcoming in *Bibliophilos*, and a poem forthcoming in Night Roses anthology *Cocktail Shaker #3*. Her poems and fiction have reached finalist status at HWG conferences. Other credits include copy for radio music shows; acknowledgements for her research and commentary in non-fiction books ranging from biographies to psychology; photographs for book and magazine covers, as well as within books, newspapers, and journals; and background slides for theater productions. She is a member of HWG and of Works in Progress.

Kevin Prufer (Warrensburg) is the author of two award-winning collections of poetry, *Strange Wood* (Carnegie Mellon UP 1998) and *The Finger Bone* (Carnegie Mellon UP 2002). His third collection, *Fallen from a Chariot*, is scheduled for publication in 2005. He co-edited (with Joy Katz) *The New Young American Poets* (Southern Illinois UP 2000) and *Dark Horses: Poets on Lost Poems* (U of Illinois P, forthcoming). He is also Editor-in-Chief of *Pleiades: A Journal of New Writing* and has work in the 2002 & 2004 *Pushcart Prize* anthologies, *Best American Poetry 2003*, *Ploughshares*, *Epoch*, *New England Review*, *Boulevard*, and *The Kenyon Review*.

Jodi Ralston (Ste. Genevieve) is pursuing a computer programming degree.

Jeanie Stewart (Hayti) is the author of several award-winning short stories and fourteen books for children and young adults. She is a member of the HWG, the Missouri Writer's Guild, and the Society of Children's Book Writers and Illustrators (SCBWI).

Donna Volkenannt (St. Peters) works full-time as a management analyst for the Department of Defense. Her work has appeared in *Saint Louis Events Magazine*, *A Cup of Comfort for Women*, and *Voyages 2000*. One of her short stories won Honorable Mention in the 4th Annual Steinbeck Short Story Competition. She has a short story forthcoming in *Storyteller Magazine*.

C. J. Winters (Blue Springs) is the author of several books (each in electronic and paperback) published or forthcoming from Hard Shell Word Factory: *Moon Night*, 1999 (2nd place Best Book award, Missouri Writers' Guild 2000); *Sleighride*, 2001 (3rd place Best Romance Novel, Missouri Writers' Guild 2002); *A Star in the Earth*; *Show-Me Murder*, *Right Man, Wrong Time*, *Mai's Ties* (women's fiction); and *Autumn* in Cranky Otter series, paranormal women's fiction/historical and contemporary romance. She has various short stories forthcoming in anthologies.